THE STARS MY REDEMPTION

by Tony Healey

About The Author:

Tony Healey is a Sussex-based writer who runs www.fringescientist.com. He was a contributor to the first Kindle All-Stars short story anthology, *Resistance Front*, along with award-winning authors Alan Dean Foster, Harlan Ellison and 30 others.

He has also contributed a piece of flash fiction to the anthology *100 Horrors*. As well as his writing, he's interviewed numerous figures in the publishing world for his site, including Bernard Schaffer, Meg Gardiner, Alan Dean Foster, Debbi Mack, Russell Brooks and many, many more.

Tony designed the Kindle All-Stars logo, and the book covers for *Distant Machines* by Simon John Cox, and *Strangers* by David Hulegaard.

He is happily married and has three daughters.

Tony can be contacted at his personal site www.tonyhealey.com or by email tonyleehealey@gmail.com

Praise For The Work Of Tony Healey:

"Tony is just one of the coolest people out there in the independent publishing world" - Bernard Schaffer, author of Whitechapel, Superbia, The Guns of Seneca 6 and other bestsellers.

"As I read, I can almost see Mr. Healey leaning in over his keyboard and salivating as he visualises himself there right next to Abe in his crazy adventures..." - David Hulegaard, author of Noble, Strangers, and Noble: Bloodlines.

"... A hurtling runaway train of sci-fi adventure!" - Simon John Cox, author of The Restoration Man, Distant Machines, and two as-yet un-published novels.

"Fun, snappy and action-filled... puts me in mind of the pulp sci-fi I've always loved, but with more panache..." - Keri Knutson, author of Darker By Degree, Director's Cut, and other bestsellers.

"Brutally competent, he's a science fiction anti-hero in the finest tradition... like I said, the story is fun!" - Richard Roberts, author of Wild Children, Sweet Dreams Are Made Of Teeth, Quite Contrary, and others.

"I like the over-the-top, B-movie, not-quite-pulp style..." - Laurie Laliberte, Editor for The Kindle All-Stars, which seeks to offer professional editing and marketing services to independent authors.

"This is the best writing Tony Healey has done so far as a science fiction author, the best storytelling, and best quality of format. This kind of writing and storytelling puts him up there with the best science fiction

authors of our time... comparable to the kind of quality produced by Steven Spielberg or M. Knight Shyamalan..." - Customer Review, Amazon.com

"Burial is an old fashioned nail biter. The prose is tinged with humor, then desperation... the writing is so good and the story scary-fun... I'd like to see an anthology of Healey's short stories." - Top 500 Customer Reviewer, Amazon.com

Copyright, Tony Healey

THE STARS MY REDEMPTION

ISBN 978-1-4717-2006-2

Copyright Tony Healey 2012

www.tonyhealey.com

AUTHOR'S NOTE

The Stars My Redemption was edited by Laurie Laliberte, of the Kindle All-Stars. The Kindle All-Stars offer professional level author services at affordable prices.

Why not check them out at www.kindleallstars.com

ACKNOWLEDGEMENTS

I'd like to say a few brief words of thanks to several people. Firstly, to my wife for allowing me the time to sit and write. Secondly, a big thanks to those who've supported my writing from the beginning: Laurie Laliberte, David Hulegaard, Richard Roberts, Keri Knutson, Simon Cox, James Harwood, Laura Macias, Natasha Whearity, to name but a few.

And last but not least, a huge debt of gratitude to author Bernard Schaffer. You've put together an incredible group of talent in the Kindle All-Stars. A group that's going to get bigger and better as time goes on. Without you bringing us together, I wouldn't have treated my writing as anything more than a hobby. I certainly wouldn't have completed anything.

So for that, for everything... thanks. Thanks to all of you.

And to everyone else? Blame this lot. They made me do it.

Tony Healey, 2012.

For Lesley

x

"Tiger, tiger, burning bright,
In the forests of the night"
- *The Tiger, William Blake*

"It was beauty killed the beast"
- *Carl Denham*

1.

Abe's ship sped like a bullet through space.

"Unidentified vessel, correct your course to one-eight-seven and slow to Galactic Standard!" the voice shouted at him. Abe pushed the thruster controls as far as they could go, grimacing. The enormous energy of the engines made the little ship rock from side to side. Above him the vast white expanse of the Union Battleship seemed to occupy every inch of space. Abe guessed it had to be at least the size of a moon, if not bigger... and it packed enough firepower to level an entire planet. He knew the Union Fleet had a couple of ships that size, and he knew the damage they could do.

The battleship had closed in on him the moment he entered the system, immediately ordering that he pull alongside. He knew they would pull his ship in and search it top to bottom if he let them. The containers of 4Fava crammed into his small cargo hold would be found, and that would be the end.

4Fava was illegal in just about every star system. Similarly, it was just as highly *sought after* in every system. They would either execute him on the spot or send him to some penal colony, chiselling granite with a toothpick until he met his maker. But he wasn't going to let that happen. He was a life-taker and a heart-breaker and he had no intention of breaking with tradition.

Abe diverted power to the thrusters, pushed them harder.

"Repeat: unidentified vessel! Slow your speed!"

"Yuh, right," Abe grunted under his breath.

Cycling through the on-board computer he selected the navigation screen and searched for nearby systems or astrological features he could make a Jump to. He found one. The uninhabited Hulegaard System. He waited as the computer calculated the necessary trajectory. The Jump Drive emitted a slow whine as it came to life.

"Correct your course and reduce your speed or we will open fire!" the voice shouted.

Abe leant down toward the audio pickup to respond, making double-sure he was good and clear.

"Fuck off!" he shouted into it at the top of his lungs.

He closed it off altogether. With one sharp thump of his fist, the speaker grill shattered like broken teeth.

Abe grabbed the control stick with both hands, and veered up towards the Battleship. He would attempt escape as soon as the Jump Drive was ready, but he knew to get in tight and close. Make it harder for them to lock weapons on him. Only a rookie would try to gain distance straight away.

The gun turrets along the Battleship's white hull sprayed rapid bursts of Neutron Shells. He zoomed upwards, pitching from side to side as the turrets struggled to lock onto his twisty-turny little ship. He gritted his teeth, snarling as he drew even closer to the hull of the Battleship, spinning his craft along its axis and weaving back and forth to avoid the artillery threatening to rip him apart.

The *READY* light flashed above his head. Abe veered away from the Union behemoth, executing a tight barrel roll and heading for open space. He reached up and activated the Jump Drive. At the same time as the collision alarm sounded.

Abe glanced at his sensor readout. He spotted several blips heading his way. The Battleship's missiles closed in fast. He grunted as his small ship accelerated to Jump speed. The endless sea of stars in front of him seemed to shrink back for a second and then expand outwards, enveloping his ship.

The same moment he expected the familiar sensation of making the Jump, a thunder-clap explosion erupted behind him. One of the missiles collided against the back of the ship. His ears rang and he was shoved into his seat as his ship accelerated beyond his control.

"Fuuuuuuuuck!" he managed to shout out. G-Force pressed on his chest and pinned his arms. It-

2.

-was Dr. Neary. She pulled back her hood and stepped out from behind her hired muscle. There were four of them, all armed to the teeth.

"That's right, Redd. Hands up," she ordered. She produced a pistol from within her robes. Her men took positions behind her, but their weapons remained fixed on Abe. He raised his arms slowly, hooking his hands behind the back of his head.

"Good boy," Neary said with a wry smirk.

Neary knew him as Redd and had been trying to track him down using that name.

She didn't realise that once he was done with a job, he was done with the name, too. His notorious anonymity was his only identifying mark. But Neary *did* have one advantage over others who tried to track

Abe down. She knew every scar and tattoo upon his body. In all her medical experience, she'd never seen someone so superficially disfigured. To most he looked like a hideous clay sculpture only purporting to be a man. A walking patchwork quilt of different bits and pieces, ripped apart and sewn back together, his face a spider's web of scar tissue hidden beneath a criss-crossed blur of tattoos.

Abe grinned at Neary as she looked him up and down. His left eye was clouded over a milky blue colour from years before, when a sonic grenade exploded mere feet from him. The force of it blew his left arm clean off, and damaged his eye. He paid a lot of money to a back-alley doctor on Galvian III to fix a cybernetic prosthesis to the stump where his arm had been, but nothing could be done with his eye. Not unless he wanted something plugged into his head that allowed him to see only in infra-red and x-rays.

With his hands behind his head, he flexed the fingers of his artificial appendage.

He never regretted the replacement of his own flesh with metal. Its unbelievable strength and durability had saved his life on more than a few occasions.

"I underestimated you, Doc," he said.

Neary laughed sarcastically. Her gun remained fixed on him, her finger on the trigger. "Yes you did," she said. "You thought I'd gone up with that ship, along with the rest of the crew, didn't you?"

"I watched it blow," he said, "T'was *beautiful* I tell yuh."

"The crew didn't deserve it..." she said, her expression changing to one of pain. Tears formed in her eyes.

Abe didn't look away. He said nothing, maintained eye contact.

"Why did you do it, Redd?" she shouted at him, "Why were you so happy for me to roast along with them? We did as you asked, didn't we? I thought we had a connection-"

"Yuh, well, I guess you had that one wrong," Abe sniggered. "Don't mistake a bit of cock for *love*, pet."

She took a step closer, her gun hand trembling. The four men stepped up and closed in.

"You really *are* an ugly son-of-a-bitch," she spat at him.

He flinched as if she'd swiped him. "Ooh, careful Doc! I'll start booing-up in a minute."

Neary signalled to one of the men who then stepped forward and swung his rifle into Abe's gut. It knocked the wind out of him and he doubled over with a grimace.

"Yuh bedside manner was better last time I saw yuh, Doc," he said as he straightened.

Neary stepped forward, swung her gun hand at the side of his face and split his lip. "See if that improves your looks!" she shouted at him.

Abe spat blood onto the floor.

"So who yuh working for?" he demanded.

"The Union, actually. They were the reason I survived your betrayal," Neary said.

"How d'yuh figure?" Abe said, frowning.

"I left the ship, even though you told me to stay with the others, and I was arrested by Union police. Then I saw the explosion as the Argayle went up. So I made a deal to help them find you."

Abe had never paid much heed to his appearance. He knew what he was, and how he appeared to others, and it didn't bother him. But to someone like Neary, his ugliness was a means of identifying him. The Union didn't have a name to go by, but they had a face – thanks to Neary. She remembered the small details in his appearance and over the months had worked with the Union to track him down.

He scowled at her, now starting to feel that familiar fire within himself. The kind where he found himself capable of anything and everything.

"Poisonous bitch!" he hissed at her.

Neary looked up as a sonic boom rattled in the sky above. Abe glanced up in time to see a Union transport entering the atmosphere, its running lights winking in the black night sky.

"Not long now, Redd. And you know what? It looks like I'll be getting my cut after all."

She signalled for her men to close in on him. One of them brought out handcuffs.

"Hold out your hands, Redd," Neary said, smiling. "Time to take you in."

Abe nodded obediently. He held out his hands, looking down at them as he did, and-

3.

-they are bloodied as he moves through the interior of the ship.

The blood isn't his.

There is no lighting in the tight corridors of the cruiser. He's made sure of that. In a way that denies his sheer size and bulk, he runs through its dark, silent innards.

A scream echoes up from far behind. He hears shouting. They must have found the body. Next to the body they will find the place where he's smashed through the cover of the influx valve with his bare hands, tearing the wiring and circuits out.

When he got caught in the act by one of the crew Abe knocked him to the floor and stove his head in against the deck plating with several powerful shakes of his giant hands.

Abe tears forward, his face set like a gargoyle's. He approaches the entrance to the front command module. He ducks past overhead piping and conduits before reaching its entrance.

He yanks the bulkhead door open. Springs through it. A quick glance around confirms what he's seen on the schematics: a central command station, where the skipper sits, and four manned stations further forward.

He moves quickly. The skipper rises from his seat, surprise stamped on his face. Abe sweeps toward him, landing a punch to his temple and twisting his hips into the hit. The man's head flies sideward and smacks against the console. Abe doesn't pause to watch him slide to the floor, as he rushes the two in front and grabs them by the hair. A fine spray of warm head-blood hits him as he smashes their skulls together and drops them back into their seats like dolls.

One of the officers at the end console stands, lifting a pistol from a holster at his side. Abe leaps at him like a tiger, latches onto his body and tumbles with him over his console and onto the floor. The pistol fires as they land, the laser bolt hitting the inside of the ship's hull with a zing. As they scramble, Abe manages to wrestle the pistol free. The officer thrashes at Abe with his soft fists.

"Sorry fella," Abe grunts, jams the barrel of the pistol into the man's ribs and fires. Abe gets up, wipes the officer's blood from his face. He spots the last officer running for the exit. He chases after him, but the man has already disappeared into the dark of the corridor. Abe slams the door shut and throws the locking wheel, sealing it from within. It'll buy him time.

He walks to the central command terminal. All of its displays are fully functional and lit up.

Behind him he hears the unmistakable sound of a plasma torch making its first incision into the metal bulkhead. A loud hollow clonk rings out from the bulkhead and he hears muffled shouting from the other side of it. Just as he expected, the officer who fled has called in the cavalry. If the engineering section is the heart of the ship then the command module is the head... and they will do whatever to win it back.

He turns back to the task at hand, working the different console controls, accessing the ammunition settings. Within moments, he finds the command sequence needed for jettisoning the cruiser's ATA-K Missiles. He needs authorisation to activate the command, a problem he anticipated. Leaning down to his side and pulling the dead skipper back up by the arm, he presses the thumb of the Captain's limp left hand to the front of the console.

"Cheers, bud," he mutters under his breath.

The controls flash and there's a slight vibration below decks as the missiles eject into space. He shoves the skipper's corpse away.

A fiery blast of energy erupts through the bulkhead, melting through the four inches of solid steel like a knife cutting butter.

Abe speaks into a small comm unit on his wrist.

"Redd to Argayle. Get into position."

He reaches into his pockets. In each hand he holds a charge rigged with a delay. He depresses their control switches and tosses them to the front of the command module where they land below the front display screens. He runs to the back of the module and presses himself against the wall. Stuffing foam buds into his ears, he takes several deep breaths, and squeezes his eyes shut. There are a few empty seconds where there is only silence and the beat of his heart.

The charges erupt in a bright white flash, sending the outer hull with it. The vacuum's pull sucks the force of the blast into space.

Abe is ripped through the hull's opening. He feels the exposed atmosphere from

*within the module rush past him. The void's
extreme freeze bites into his skin in the
seconds it takes him to hurtle from the
destroyed bow of the cruiser into the
waiting cargo bay of his own ship. He hits
the floor of the hold hard as the cargo bay
doors immediately slam shut behind him.
The life support systems work to fill the bay
with fresh, breathable air.*

*Abe's body burns all over and his veins
feel like they're pumping hot lava. He
inhales, keeps his eyes shut. Abe knows all
too well that opening them too soon after
exposure could result in permanent
damage. He's seen men bleed from their
pupils following an unintended space walk.*

*A hand falls on his shoulder. Someone
kneels next to him. He feels the pinch of an
injection in his upper arm. Fingers dig
inside his ears and pull the buds out.*

*"I'm going to give you immediate
treatment and then get you to the med bay,"
a soft voice says.*

It's Dr. Neary. Her hand goes to his head, stroking his temple.

The shot she's given him starts to work. The burning vanishes. Neary keeps talking but her voice is distant, receding down a tunnel.

"Lorna..." he croaks groggily – sleepily – before everything goes black.

4.

Abe wakes to blinding lights. He holds up a hand to shield his eyes. A blurry figure stands to his right. As his vision clears, he sees it's Neary. He could have picked anybody to handle communications duties, but he needed someone able to give him immediate medical care too. Neary fit the bill.

She lays a hand on him reassuringly.

"How long have I been out?" he asks her.

"A few hours," she says, pulling a cannula from his wrist. "That was a risky move you did back there."

"Haven't done it in a while," he says, "Feeling groggy."

Neary laughs.

"You said 'I have to go Lorna' before you zonked out earlier. Who is that? A girlfriend?"

Abe licks his lips.

"A girl I, uh, used to know," he says.

Just thinking about her makes him forget what he's up to, makes him dismiss whatever immoral deed he's indulging in. Anything to do with her makes him feel guilty in a way that he could never explain away.

Neary shrugs at his explanation, nonplussed. "Well, you've taken well to the treatment, anyway. Another few hours and you'll be back to normal," she says. Her hand finds his, caresses it, making circles on his rough skin.

"I knew you were the right doc for the job."

"The best," Neary says.

Abe tries to sit up but finds that he can't move. His muscles are stiff knots. He grimaces as he flops back to the bed.

"Rest. Don't try to get up just yet. Lay flat," Neary says.

She steps away for a second and he turns his head to see her close the door to the unit and lock it. She pulls the blinds.

"The others are stowing away the missiles in the hold. Everything's gone to plan. You have to relax."

"Yuh..." he says.

She bends down and her smooth, full lips touch his. As they kiss, Neary reaches over and turns the lights off. Abe finds that even though he can't get up, there is still a part of him that can, and he pulls her to him, denying the throbbing of his muscles. As he kisses her he takes her hand and places it on his member to let her know he's ready.

He feels the steady thrum of the ships engines beneath him as they couple. The Argayle will be headed toward the K-Clarke System. There they will rendezvous with the buyer, the leader of some Tezzerite revolutionary group. It doesn't matter to

Abe who buys the missiles, so long as somebody does. As long as he gets paid.

Of course, Neary is attractive too.

Most women find his physical appearance off-putting... his scars, the roughness of his skin. His heavily muscled frame. The majority of women look at him with repulsion. There are some, however, who seem to like the way he looks, for whatever reason, and Neary has been giving him the eye since the day they met.

Now they are in the full-flow of sex. She climbs on top of him, her hands on his chest as she rises up and down upon him, back and forth. She sucks his nipples, biting them in-between groans as she quickens her pace on top of him, reaching orgasm.

"Lorna..." he whispers, his eyes closed, the name slipping out before he can stop it. Dr. Neary doesn't hear him. She's moaning in ecstasy, leant back on him, her breasts solid and hard, one hand on his chest and the fingers of the other running through her damp hair as she cums.

Despite his aching muscles he throws back his head, arching off of the bed, his eyes rolling into their sockets as he finishes at the same time as her.

"... Lorna..." he almost whispers again, breathless.

5.

Afterward, when she's cleaned herself up and left him to rest, he lays on the bed smiling. He knows what Neary's up to. It's not the first time a woman on a team he's put together has used him for a bigger cut than the others. He respects it. In his experience women can be cunning, ruthless creatures. Instead of anger at her ulterior motives, he feels pleased that she's making moves on him to better her position. Perhaps she truly finds him repulsive, just like all the others. Perhaps it is all an act. But with the lights off she has undoubtedly forgotten that repulsion and enjoyed herself. Judging from the throbbing of his subsiding erection he's pretty sure she did.

Now that he has slept with her he knows she will try to convince him that she is worth more than her agreed percentage.

And he will agree to it... because he has no plans of splitting the money anyway. As always he will make the sale personally. He'll collect the cash and then disappear. His team knows him as Redd, and that's only one in a long list of names he's used over the years.

He accumulates pseudonyms as a magpie collects bits of shiny paper. Over the years there've been hundreds. Prospective employers know him only by the fact that he does not have a name. He has a reputation for being all at once cut-throat, ruthless, murderous... and anonymous. And that's how he likes it. His employers always manage to find him, regardless of what he calls himself. After all, it isn't his name they employ, it's his reputation. He doesn't care for names.

They're disposable, like clothing. Forgettable.

But nobody ever forgets him...

Abe puts his hands behind his head and looks up at the ceiling, finally relaxing.

He'll make the sale and collect on what he's owed, then he'll split. Wasn't it he who risked the void for it? The missiles are worth a fortune. Doesn't he deserve it? When he's able to get up and about, he'll make his way below decks as the others sleep and remove one of the warheads from a missile. He'll stow it near the engines, hidden from sight, and set it to detonate an hour or so after he's left to make the sale. The ship isn't his anyway, he's just told the crew it is. He borrowed it from someone back on Schaffer IV.

Neary will get a bigger piece than she hoped for when the ship blows with all of them on it. He only wishes he could be nearby to watch. He hopes he will be, but most likely he'll be long-gone by the time it goes off.

Abe closes his eyes to get some sleep.

Neary will be back in a few hours for another go-around; he knows it.

He lays there and waits-

6.

-for the guy with the cuffs to come near his hands and then he sprang into action.

Abe grabbed him by the wrists and went in with a headbutt. Claret splattered all over his face as the guy's nose shattered. Neary fired, and Abe used the man as a human shield, holding him in front and then charging forward, knocking her over before she could fire again. Two came at Abe, one on either side. He swung his bionic left arm backwards, hitting the one on the left in the neck and sending the man staggering backwards, gasping for breath. The other guy managed to grab Abe's right arm, but Abe spun about, smashing him full force in the chest with his metal fist.

The man dropped to the floor and as he did, Abe kicked him in the side of the head.

"Lights out," he grunted.

He turned toward the fourth goon, who stood back and levelled his weapon, preparing to fire. Abe pointed his bionic arm at the thug, a small compartment on its surface lifted up. He fired two small darts and goon-number-four looked down, astonished, as they struck him in the mid-section. Abe dived onto the floor and covered his head with his hands as seconds later the darts exploded, sending flesh, blood and cartilage everywhere. He didn't wait around. He got up and started running as the body parts rained down around him, splatting onto the sandy ground.

Behind him he heard Neary scream.

He spared a glance back at her as he ran, and caught sight of the Doctor smothered in blood, screaming hysterically.

"See yuh 'round, doc," he called back to her, chuckling as he ran into the night towards the canyon where he'd hidden his ship. By the time they determined the direction he'd fled, he was long gone. Or so he thought when-

7.

-the ship shuddered. Every light flashed red and he could only guess at the damage the missile had caused. If it had hit full on it would have incinerated him altogether. He heard the whistle of precious atmosphere escaping into the vacuum from a hull breach somewhere around him.

The force of the Jump pinned him to his seat. He couldn't even move his arms.

Through the glass of the cockpit the stars hurtled past, and then everything changed from passing starlight to bright fiery orange, as if he were passing through the heart of a sun. He knew that if that were the case he'd be dead already. From what he could see of the readouts on his screen he'd exited the Jump directly into the upper atmosphere of a planet and now his ship rocked uncontrollably towards the planet's surface.

Fighting the weight of inertia as he fell planetward, he reached towards the control console with his bionic arm to engage the emergency air brakes. They deployed at the sides of the craft.

Still, he knew he was going too fast.

WARNING* *UNCONTROLLED BURN flashed on the screen.

The pressure eased a little as the ship hit air resistance, Abe was finally able to move both arms. He grabbed the control stick and tried to bring the nose up to level his descent. He managed a few degrees but the ship was mostly unresponsive. The flame of the ionised atmosphere peeled back to reveal the planet beneath. A barren, white, frozen wasteland that stretched as far as he could see in all directions.

"Hell," he grunted, fighting for just a few more degrees out of her, "*Fucking hell.*"

He was coming in far too hot, far too fast. Normally he'd have ejected but the ship didn't have that functionality. He had it removed to make more room for smuggling materials.

The ground rushed up to meet him and he continued pulling on the control stick with all his strength, trying to level her out a bit. He passed over a series of snowy peaks, towards a wide open stretch of the frozen tundra.

Abe gripped the arms of his seat, flinched instinctively as the craft met the ground. The belly of the ship peeled away as if it were skin. It thundered along the ice, the metal screamed as it tore away. The ship shuddered to a stop, grated along the hard ground and slid sidewards. Abe was thrown forward in his seat, hitting his head on the metal flight console. Sparks flew in front of his eyes. He felt the warm trickle of blood down his face.

His vision swam. The ship lay on its side. Smoke poured from the front and washed over the cockpit. It burned the back of his throat, choking him. His legs pulsed with pain and he saw that part of the console had collapsed above his knees, pinning them in tight.

Gotta get out, he thought.

He felt exhausted, yet still he unbuckled his harness and reached down to hold the collapsed console in both hands. His iron muscles strained as he pulled upwards with all of his might, clenching his teeth so hard they threatened to crack. The metal twisted up away from his legs long enough for him to pull them free.

Coughing, his eyes burning from the smoke, he wrenched open the top hatch of the cockpit and lifted himself out. His legs throbbed as he spilled out over the side of the ship and onto the snow.

He staggered up and started moving. He didn't know where he was, and he didn't know if the Union had tracked his wild ride toward the planet. For all he knew they might already be on their way. He ran across the snow, using reserves of energy that wouldn't have existed in any other man.

After twenty or so minutes, however, the freezing temperatures began to take their toll on him, and he was forced to slow. With only his flight suit on he had minimal insulation against the external temperature. His legs and chest ached, and he was panting. Blinking to clear his vision, he scanned the featureless terrain for something – *anything* – he could use for survival. There was nothing.

I think I'm fucked.

His feet dragged and his legs burned. He pumped them like a mad man, the smoking hulk of his broken ship receding into the distance. Another time he might have continued on that way for hours. But he'd been through a lot within a few hours, and he was feeling it now.

He looked up and spotted something ahead, on the horizon.

Movement.

Slowing down, he tried to make out what it was through the blood pounding in his ears and the hum settling like static over his brain. It was the unmistakable silhouette of people coming his way.

They've seen the ship, he thought. *Whoever they are, they know I've arrived.*

Abe carried on toward them until he stumbled and fell forward in the snow, finally exhausted. He had no weapon on him, nothing but the flight suit. He wished he'd thought to grab one now. He felt the freeze now, creeping inside his suit, wrapping its icy tendrils about his body and burning his skin.

He lifted his head out of the snow and looked up, trying to make out who they were. What planet was it? If it was un-populated then they were either pirates hiding from the Union, or they were savages.

He tried to get up. His limbs gave way, and he flopped the snow again. He tumbled to his side. His eyes lolled in his head as he fought to remain conscious. His head swam. Everything felt distant.

He was reminded of the deck of the Argayle, after braving the vacuum and of the sensation of going away, of slipping.

"Gahhh..." he groaned.

Again, Abe tried to move, but it was futile. His batteries were drained. Nothing left.

He laid on his back in the snow. He looked up at the sky, and at first he thought night was closing in then he realised he was blacking out.

"I can..." he mumbled, not quite knowing what he was saying. As he closed his eyes he saw her face, like something ancient from the seabed churned up by the tide. A part of his memory he'd tried so often to repress, to no avail.

A face, a name, a feeling within him that kept cropping up when he least expected it... or needed it. As he fell, he reached for her in his mind.

"... Lorna..."

The cold knocked him out completely, and by the time they arrived he was barely alive.

8.

Abe was moving. His eyelids fluttered open and he found himself floating under a big blue sky free from clouds. Something or someone carried him. His arms were pinned by his sides, but he felt some soft of fabric, maybe canvas, beneath his fingertips. There was a heavy fur throw over him. He looked to the side and saw several men and women walking alongside all in furs.

A hand fell to his shoulder and Abe looked up. A man walked to the other side of him and peered down inquisitively.

"Rest. We found you in the snow," the man said in a strong, firm voice.

"What planet is this?" Abe asked.

"Rest," the man said again.

Abe gave up and closed his eyes.

9.

There is darkness again, and he floats within it.

No stars. Just black. A deep, sumptuous nothingness that swallows him up, enfolding and consuming him. Abe sinks within it, as if it were a heavy ocean of oil. And then there is warmth, rising up from the deep.

The heat grows in intensity and becomes fire, burning his flesh.

Abe is back on Ryana, fighting his way through the fires raging in the capital city. He is younger than he is now, much younger. He has not seen and done the things that have left him broken and bitter. Abe fights his way through the populace, choking on the burning air and trying to force his way to the front of the mob. The entire city is burning, and everyone is evacuating. He was brought to Ryana as an orphan child. Now he leaves as a similarly orphaned adult.

The heat turns to wet humidity.

Abe is hiking across the jungles of Alannaris as a Union soldier. It has been five years since Ryana. There was a dogfight in the upper atmosphere and he was shot down. Now he makes tracks through the thick vegetation in an attempt to get to some kind of higher ground. He hopes they'll be able to detect the signal from the tracking device implanted within his neck. The air is thick and moist and it is hard to breathe. Abe just thanks his lucky stars that the Alannarians haven't found him yet. At the back of his mind he wonders if the tracking device even works, and whether they'll even bother to try and find him. In fact he wonders if the Alannarians will detect it first. He is still young, and very much inexperienced.

I don't want to die alone, *he thinks.* I don't want to die here.

Abe floats within the dark. He starts to turn around and around, over and over. He does not fear death. He doesn't want to die, but he doesn't fear the inevitability of it.

Abe has left the Union army. He is lying in a dirty bed with an even dirtier woman. She kisses him after several hours of fucking. There was no lovemaking. There was no love. They have an arrangement. An agreement. Soon after, he pays her and leaves. Although he has satisfied himself, there is an empty hole opening up in the middle of him.

The hole will grow bigger over the years. Eventually it will more or less consume him.

He remembers what happened after his brief tour of duty on Vitka III.

There is a hospital bed. He is bleeding all over it. He can't feel his legs. He can't feel his feet. He can't move them. It's like they're not there.

Ice. Empty ice. He is screaming. The people around him are wearing masks. They shoot him up with something. It spreads itself cold and numbing around his body, through his heart, over his brain. The black envelops him again, pulling him back down into its steady tide.

Chabon III. Abe lines up his shot on the door of the compound. He is using a long-range Zeboscope sniper rifle. His hands are steady and sure, and he waits patiently, barely breathing. His target exits through the door, as expected. For a split second he hesitates. It's his first assassination. He squeezes off the trigger and instantaneously the target's head vaporises. He walks away calmly, but for days afterwards something about it bothers him. It was a clean, quick kill. A humane kill. He has no feelings about killing someone; that died within him years ago. But such a kill does not satisfy him. He feels nothing.

Abe rides the waves. They propel him upwards.

A grenade goes off in front of him. He is thrown backwards. The left side of his face burns as if it has been sprayed with acid. When he sits up and looks around, he sees his arm lying on the floor. There are more coming for him. The grenade has only delayed them. He leaves his severed limb and runs.

It is getting lighter. The dark recedes. His world is grey twilight.

The life-boat. At first the sex was rough and primal. But then in spending their time together it became something else. She lies next to him, hugging his chest as she sleeps. He feels weird. Something has changed within him. For the first time in years he feels uncomfortable because for the first time in years he made love.

It is getting lighter and lighter. He rises. The dark lifts him towards the light.

"Why leave me here?" she asks him. She reaches out to take his hand - his real one. He flinches back from her, resisting.

"I thought we had a connection..." she presses him.

Abe looks away.

"You'll be safe here," he says, avoiding the subject.

She doesn't say anything more, but he knows without looking at her that she is crying.

"I have to go..." he starts and then turning his back on her he walks away. Almost-dawn and he is meeting it. The night slips away.

10.

He's crying. He doesn't know where he is, when it is, who he is, or why he doesn't know these things. He just is. He is *He*.

Abe's crying. Somehow this is a strange sensation for him, something that doesn't come naturally, as if the tears are an exception, like letting yourself bleed without being cut.

"I don't know if you can hear me," a voice says.

Why can't I open my eyes?

"You're very sick. We're trying to help you. We're trying to fight the fever."

He tries to move his arms but can't. He can't be sure if it's because he's restrained in some way or if it's because he simply doesn't have the energy to lift them.

"You're in a bad way, but we're going to do everything we can," the voice says.

Had she said about a fever? He can't be sure.

It is just a voice. A voice in the darkness.

A god.

Was he crying or was he sweating? He thinks both.

They're the same, he thinks. *I don't want to shed either. But blood - that's fine. Blood is there to be shed, to be spread all over the place. In a minute I'll paint every-fucking-thing in this fucking place-wherever-it-is red!*

Something brushing past his cheek. A hand?

"You probably can't hear me anyway," the voice says, "but I'll be back in a bit to check on you. And I'll keep talking so you know somebody is here."

It's a woman's voice.

Again that face washes up from the nothingness, the smell of her hair, the touch of her hands over his body, her lips on his.

And blood. A *sea* of it, and the two of them writhing within it.

Fever! Infection!

"I won't leave your side," the voice says, but once more he is descending into the darkness.

I love you Abe.

I love you too.

11.

Abe woke to find himself in a tent. He looked around. The tent was probably twenty feet long, ten feet wide. He was connected to an IV that had murky water in it. Abe guessed it was more than fluids, perhaps containing a nutritional solution.

Next to his bed stood an empty chair and a monitor that ticked his pulse.

A stove stood on the other side of his bed, pumping out heat. He heard someone enter the tent. He tried to sit up but merely flopped back onto the bed.

He remembered this man's face. This was the man he had seen outside. He set a glass on the stand near Abe's head and stood by the bed with his hands out.

"May I?" he asked.

Abe said nothing, but nodded.

The man leaned forward cautiously and lifted Abe, propping him against his pillows in a sitting position. The man's strength, considerable for his smaller stature, surprised Abe.

He urged Abe to drink from the glass.

"Please," he said.

Abe sipped from it, warily. On any other occasion he would have knocked it out of the man's hand. It could be poison. It could be a serum intended on prying many dark, hidden truths from the blackest recesses of his soul. But he was thirsty and they'd obviously taken care of him. Abe allowed himself to relax... *just a little.*

The man wore army surplus - an outdated style Abe had only seen in old pictures. Were they soldiers? Was he on a base of some kind?

But why the old uniform?

Once Abe had his fill, the man returned the glass to the table and sat. Abe took him to be about thirty. He had jet black hair swept back over his head and dual-coloured eyes, his left eye green and his right eye blue. It was a common mutation, and a natural one, but there was something about it nagging to be remembered and Abe was groggy and not fully with it. Something about eyes of different colours...

"I'm Paul," the man said to Abe.

"Yuh," Abe grunted.

His throat was dry as dust despite the water.

"And yours?" Paul pressed.
Abe thought for a moment. Should he use another name? Start another identity with these people, even though they'd obviously saved his life?

Fuck it, he thought.

"Abe," he said finally. "Just Abe."

Paul nodded. "Nice to meet you, Abe."

"Where am I?"

"A planet within the Rishi Drift," Paul said. "You were barely alive when we

71

pulled you from the snow. We saw your ship enter the atmosphere, then we spotted the smoke from the wreckage. We went looking for survivors and found you."

Abe hadn't heard of the Rishi Drift. It certainly wasn't in the Hulegaard system that was for sure.

"How long have I been out?" Abe asked.

"About four days," Paul said. "You had a fever but we managed to fight it back. We thought we might lose you a few times though... you were pretty close to death."

I've been close to death a fair bit, Abe thought.

"Yuh, well, thanks."

Paul held up his hands. "No need to thank us. We were only doing what anyone else would have done. Mind you, if you're going to thank anyone, thank Sara when she's around. She looked after you."

"Okay. So what's the deal? Am I your prisoner?" Abe asked.

"No. Why would you think that?" Paul asked, frowning.

Abe glanced around once again. He looked down at himself. He was naked apart from the sheet covering his modesty, but he was clean. The woman Paul had mentioned had probably been bathing him whilst he was out of it. There were no restraints on the bed, and he saw no security measures, no cameras, motion sensors or energy fields... Nothing to stop him just getting up and walking out but his own weakness and lack of energy.

Still, how could he know if Paul was hiding something? Abe was a man as capable of deceit as he was of falling prey to it. Usually the moment you let your guard down was when you found yourself at the wrong end of a weapon.

"Then where am I? Is this a camp? A base? A city?"

Abe was frustrated and angry. He felt his vitality trickling back. It usually did when he got agitated. He got strength from his gut, from the fire in his belly.

Paul sat forward, his hands clasped in front of him as he explained. "We are all refugees here, if you will. There are about thirty of us... there were more when we arrived but we've lost a few along the way. You're currently about fifty feet beneath the surface, in one of a series of caves. They're the only shelter to be found for miles around, and you've seen how harsh it is up there," he said.

Abe remembered what he'd seen before he blacked out; a flat, white nothingness. He didn't doubt that the only way you could survive was beneath the surface where there was shelter.

Abe shifted on the bed impatiently. He felt stronger, more awake.

"Yuh, but *listen to me*. Am I your prisoner?" Abe insisted.

"Well put it this way, if you *are* then you're no more a prisoner than we are," Paul said.

Abe looked at him in the same way a caged animal looks at its owner when they open the door and invite them outside.

"How long have you been here?" he demanded.

"About eighteen years, give or take," Paul said.

Eighteen years!

A thousand questions raced into Abe's mind. For one thing, how had they survived for so long on such a desolate world? But there was one question that took priority over any of the others.

"You saying you're stuck here?"

Paul stood up. "I'm afraid so," he said.

Abe took a deep breath.

"And that means I am, then," he said.

"I'm very sorry," Paul said.

Abe stared dead ahead, cold and hard.

12.

He whipped back the bed sheet, swung his legs over the side. Paul made to help him but Abe waved him off.

"No," he said, easing himself onto his feet. His legs were wobbly and he felt weak, but he managed to stand away from the bed albeit swaying back and forth.

Paul handed him some clothes, and Abe put them on. He sat on the edge of the bed for a moment as he put some boots on.

He got up, flexed.

"Take it easy, you've been out of it for days. You've not had a good meal in you yet. We've only been able to get intravenous fluids and nutrients into you," Paul explained.

Abe stretched in front of him, his muscles popping and creaking.

"You shouldn't exert yourself," Paul said.

Abe ignored him. "Not going to. I gotta stretch my legs," he said as he strode outside the tent with Paul following behind.

There were a few of the "refugees" going about their business. They all looked in the direction of the tent as Paul and Abe emerged. The cave was a giant hollow within the grey rock, about a hundred feet across. In the centre Abe saw steam pumping from an opening in the floor. There were several tunnels shooting off from the cave in different directions, one of them curving upwards as it ran off from the cave, presumably toward the surface. High-intensity lights were dotted here and there, giving limited illumination.

Along with his own tent there were about ten more dwellings, spread around the cave floor. Possessions and clothes were arranged outside the tents. He could see that life here was very much communal.

"That's a thermal vent," Paul said pointing in the direction of the funnel of steam rising into the middle of the cave. "It gives just the right amount of natural heat. The airflow from the tunnels prevents a build-up of moisture in here by circulating and venting it to the surface, where it dissipates."

"Lucky," Abe remarked, looking around.

What were the chances of crash landing on a planet covered in ice and snow and sharp sub-zero winds... only to find a nice warm cave under the ground? He was surprised that it all worked as well as Paul said it did, but obviously he was right or the whole place would have been dripping wet with condensation.

The others gathered together and watched them. He saw that they wore the same old army uniform as Paul.

"Don't mind *them*," Paul said, nodding across at them. "They're just curious. You've got to remember that we've never had a visitor here before. We've lived by ourselves."

"Yuh," Abe said, thinking of those eighteen long years they'd been trapped here. Where had he been eighteen years ago? What had he been doing? He was but a boy all that time ago. A young man, fighting for what was right. Or so he had believed.

His concept of right and wrong had changed in the years since...

Abe asked Paul where the tunnels led. Regardless of the situation in which he found himself, he always adhered to his golden rule: know how to get in and how to get out. When you feel the heat around the corner, know that you can get out quick. The golden rule of any career criminal.

"That one leads back up to the surface," Paul said, pointing at the one Abe already suspected wound its way to the top. "And those lead to smaller, lesser caves. We don't have much use for those. Besides, we prefer to live together."

Abe noted the ground they walked on. "It's perfectly level," he said.

Paul nodded. "Yes it's almost too flat. We've wondered if these caves were used before we arrived, perhaps for refuge by another race. Maybe they adapted them and made the floor this way. I can't see nature leaving it flat like that."

Abe felt stiff and sore but he knew it was best for him to walk it off. *Don't just lay around, moping. Get back up. Fight, even if you're only fighting yourself. Fighting weakness.*

"So what were you all before?" Abe asked.

"We were soldiers, pilots, medics, engineers. You know, for the Union. That makes us sound like we were conscripts but we weren't... we were little more than slaves."

The other refugees looked Abe up and down, in awe of his appearance. They were all so youthful, showing none of the signs of stress he expected to see on people who'd survived on a lifeless planet for nearly two decades. Abe nodded at them in greeting. He noticed none of them tried to approach and interrupt Paul as he spoke to him. Paul was very much their figurehead.

"So yuh weren't enlisted?" he asked, frowning.

"Not in any way you'd consider us to be, no," Paul said.

"I don't follow," Abe said.

"Well, we were scattered like children when the Union ships left us behind. Panic set in. Many of us died. But for whatever reason, the rest of us... we came together," Paul said, illustrating what he was saying by meshing the fingers of his hands as he spoke.

"You were abandoned?" Abe asked. What Paul was saying rang a bell somewhere at the back of his mind, "I was in the army myself around that time..."

Paul shot him a look. "Did you ever get assigned to Massa E Kym?"

"Yuh, but..." Abe looked first at Paul then the faces of the men and women around them. Now he remembered the significance of Paul's dual-coloured eyes. He turned in a circle and saw that they all had it. One blue eye, one green. The men and women in front of him were all different shapes, sizes, skin colours... and yet they had that one unifying feature.

Now it struck home.

The bells weren't just ringing. They crashed in atomic-brass-explosions.

Replicants. They were all replicants. That was why they were left for dead. So they really *were* refugees.

Union Replicants, a fighting force manufactured for the battlefield. In all respects they were human, aside from the fact that they were produced with dual-coloured eyes so that they could be distinguished from bona-fide Terrans. Right down to the genetic level, they were perfect replications of human beings. However, despite the fact that for all intents and purposes they were human, that was not how they were viewed or treated by the Union.

"I can see that you've just realised *who* and *what* we are, haven't you?" Paul asked, studying his face.

"I was there," Abe said, looking away in thought. "I saw who was left behind."

Massa E Kym, he thought. *Fuck.*

"You were left for dead," he said, almost disbelieving.

Paul started introducing the others to him, throwing names his direction that he'd never remember without asking for them again. As he grunted greetings and thanks to them all in turn, he noted how they hailed from many different flavours of humanity; Asian, African, Hispanic, Martian... and yet they each had a blue and a green eye, unifying them as much as the mutual dilemma of being marooned where they were.

A dark-haired woman with creamy white skin approached him out of the crowd. She was slim but curvy. As she drew near she greeted him with a smile.

"This is Sara. She's been looking after you. She's the only medically-trained person here," Paul said, introducing her.

"Well, the *only* one left now," Sara corrected him.

"Yes. Of course. Sorry."

"Hiya," Abe said, cutting in.

"Nice to finally see you up and about," Sara said, offering her hand. Abe took it, small delicate, into his own giant mechanical mitt.

"All thanks to you, doc," he said, conjuring up a grin.

She looked him over.

"How are you feeling?"

"Alright, s'pose," he said.

"Eaten yet?" she asked him.

Abe shook his head. Now that he thought about it, he did feel hungry. They'd had a drip in him for days, but that didn't make up for not having a proper meal. He felt weak and wobbly on his feet, but not so much that he felt the need to mention it to her.

"I did say for him to take it easy," Paul chirped in.

Abe grimaced. "I don't like to lay in bed. Gotta get up. Gotta get moving about. It's how I've always been. It's my way."

Sara looked about and then waved one of the others away from a bench in front of one of the tents. She led him with her hand at the small of his back.

"*Sit*. Don't move," she said.

He grunted in frustration but sat, regardless. He'd never argue with a doctor, despite the fact that his last encounter with one had evolved into a bit of a tricky situation...

Abe sat down on the bench, secretly glad to be off his feet. His head was swimming. He hadn't felt so physically impaired for a long, long time. Paul continued to mingle with the others, chatting. Sara returned to him with a bowl of something hot.

"Here. Eat this," she said.

He took it from her. It didn't look all that appetising. Abe held the bowl up to his nose and sniffed it, unsure.

"It's a kind of soup," Sara said to him, "Just eat it."

He cocked an eyebrow at her.

"Yes Ma'am," he said mockingly, lifting the bowl to his lips and drinking the gloopy concoction without fuss; it wasn't that bad, he found. A little bland, but it was hot and filled a hole. Whatever was in it obviously had a high nutritional content, because once he'd finished he started to feel better. He handed the empty bowl back to her.

"Better?" she asked him.

Abe nodded. "Yuh," he said, meaning it.

"Paul's right. You should have rested a bit longer, maybe had something to eat before getting up and about."

Abe said nothing.

He watched Paul speak to the others. From his body language and the way he interacted with them, he was obviously telling them to give him some space and get back to their own business for the time being. He seemed to be worried about overwhelming Abe... but that wasn't the case. He was weak. He was thrown by the fact that he'd awakened from days of fighting a fever in his sleep to find himself marooned on a lump of ice with a band of runaway slaves. But overwhelmed? Not in the slightest.

In fact, one of the first things he'd thought was, *What about the 4Fava?* If his ship was still intact, then what about his cargo? Did it still sit there waiting for him to collect it, or had they removed it? He decided to tread carefully with these "refugees." Drug trafficking wasn't exactly a regular occupation for him, but it was one he had no inhibitions against. His conscience was clear.

If the idiots want to shoot that shit into their bodies let 'em, he thought.

Regardless, the replicants might not feel the same way and it could cause problems. They probably didn't have a clue what it was anyway, if they *had* seen what was on his ship.

If they didn't know yet about the 4Fava then he didn't want them to know. It might cause confrontation between him and them. After they saved his life, he'd feel rotten if he had to harm any of them. If he could get away with it, he'd prefer to not let the tiger out of the cage. Unless he was forced to. If they stood between him and what was his, then he didn't hold himself responsible for the consequences.

Abe looked Sara over as she turned her head to see where Paul had gone. She was beautiful, and not in any glamorous, fake way like most of the women he'd come across. He saw that she was naturally beautiful, even when dressed in ill-fitting army surplus. That she was a replicant in origin didn't bother him in the slightest, and the idea that she was somehow different wasn't a notion he even entertained.

He'd been with replicants. He'd been with aliens. Women were women.

She turned back to him.

"I take it I was in a bad way then," Abe said.

"You were. And I nearly lost you, too," she said. "By the way, you kept calling something every time you broke through the fever. A name..."

"Yuh?" he asked, squinting up at her. Regarding her through his milky white eye gave her an angelic, misty outline.

"Luana? Lana?" Sara said, "Something like that. You were calling it over and over again. Does that mean anything to you? Is it someone you know?"

Abe hung his head slightly and looked down at his hands where they hung in his lap, one real over the one constructed from metal.

Lorna.

"I knew her once," he said, and then after a beat, "But that was in the past."

"I see," Sara said a little uncomfortably.

Abe looked up.

"Sorry love," he tapped the side of his skull, "Ghosts in the shell."

Paul emerged from the crowd carrying a set of big, thick furs. He handed one of them to Abe.

"Here, put this on. It won't keep all the cold out, but it'll stop you freezing to death while we're outside."

Abe stood up and put it on.

"Where are we going?"

Paul nodded ahead of them to the tunnel that twisted its way to the surface.

"*Up*. There's something you should see. If you're up to it, of course?"

Abe nodded in acknowledgement. Sara tutted. Paul put a hand on her shoulder.

"Sorry Sara. Only if you agree of course," he said.

She rolled her eyes. "I'm fine with it, so long as you're not too long in that cold. If he starts to go funny, you drag him back down here," she said to Paul.

"I will," Paul said.

"Don't yuh worry, doc," Abe said. "I'm sure he'll look after me."

She stood with her hands poised on her hips, watching them go.

13.

"They call us replicants but for all intents and purposes we're just as human as you are," Paul said as they started up the tunnel, a steep incline of frozen grey rock and thick, glassy ice. "Obviously we differ in certain ways. Some of our race are brought into being entirely obedient. Following instructions like robots. They never see their full potential as individuals because, frankly, they don't have any. They're just limited."

Abe noticed the word *race* when Paul talked about his people. He thought that perhaps his view of things was right. Although they'd been created, manufactured by manipulating the genome, they were somehow an off-shoot of man that *man* had created. Humanity had *brought them into being*, and Abe wondered if Paul considered his creators akin to gods...

"I know the type," Abe said, "they were the soldiers fighting on the frontline. They were fearless."

"Yes. But only because they didn't know any different," Paul said. The tunnel grew suddenly steep, so much so that it was almost unwalkable. Paul leant forward to get some purchase on the ice. The path became a kind of ledge, and once he was up he offered Abe his hand to help him get up and over. Abe accepted it. With his other hand he grabbed the edge of the ice shelf and jumped up with his feet. It was not the effortless move Paul made, and Abe landed roughly on his knees.

"Are you okay?" Paul asked him.

"Yuh," he said. He felt drained from the exertion of climbing up onto the ledge.

"Just rest here a moment, Abe," Paul said, "There's no rush."

Abe didn't have a choice; he *had* to stop from sheer fatigue. He got up off the floor and stood against the tunnel wall. He knew it was best for a man to be on his feet.

"We've been away for nearly twenty years. Has much changed?" Paul asked him.

Abe considered for a moment whilst he caught his breath. "If you're asking if the Union is still making soldiers, then yuh, they are."

Paul shook his head in disgust. "I'd hoped someone would have seen the barbarity of it and tried to stop it by now," he said. "Creating life for the sake of it."

The corner of Abe's mouth lifted in a slanted grin.

"Look, bud, you're talking about a massive power at war with an equally massive power. The average man doesn't want fuck all to do with the war. They're staying clear. And yuh know what? Don't blame 'em either, mate. Look at me. I got outta there as soon as I could. But the trouble is, if there ain't nobody signing up to fight on the frontline then they've gotta have someone else doing it. That's where you lot come in," Abe said nodding at him.

"So you agree with it," Paul said.

"*No*. I never said that. I think that all they've done is create human slaves. They call it a fighting force, and they like to say that you're not really human," Abe thumbed back in the direction of the main cave, "But from what I've seen, there ain't nothing *inhuman* about yuh. You look and act like the real McCoy, as far as I can tell, and the way you're living is human enough. I've never agreed with what they've done, and I'm a man who's done a lot of disagreeable things in my time. Trust me."

"I'm glad to hear you have that outlook," Paul said.

Abe shrugged. "That's how I see it. But you gotta remember that you owe your existence to those Union scientists," Abe said. "So it's a bit like having a whore for a Mother and a psycho for a Dad. You might not agree with 'em, but hey, that's yuh lot in life."

Paul sniggered. "That's a very colourful way of putting it," he said.

"Look. The Draxx enslave races, right? All the worlds of the third quarter? Enslaved. And I'm not saying it's a terrible thing. But then consider the Union. Fuck sake, they just grow their slaves. What's worse? What's more unforgivable? It got to a point where I didn't see a difference between us and them. That's when I did a runner and went my own way."

Paul regarded him with understanding eyes. "Much like us, only in different circumstances. You look like a man who's made his own way in life," he said.

"I have. And I've lived by my own rules. Might be that some don't agree with how I live my life. Don't agree with my existence. But there's a lot of people don't agree with yours either."

"That's true," Paul said.

Abe stood away from the tunnel wall and continued slowly trudging his way forward. Any other time he would have sprinted up the tunnel. He paused again and turned around.

"Yuh know, seems to me we're in the same boat mate," Abe said.

14.

Paul led him out onto the snow. A few yards from the tunnel entrance there were two oblong objects covered in sheeting, about three metres long, two metres wide, and anchored to the frozen ground by chains. From the way they swayed to and fro, Abe could see they were older model anti-grav platforms. *Skimmers*. Paul walked to the nearest one and pulled off the sheet.

"We're not walking then," Abe remarked with a chuckle.

Paul took the sheeting and threw it through the entrance to the tunnel to prevent the wind blowing it away, then set about unhooking the anchor.

"We have three of them. We found them not long after crashing here," Paul said.

"Found them?" Abe asked.

Paul cast the chains to one side and climbed aboard. He motioned for Abe to follow suit. As Abe got up, several large icicles that hung from the edge of the platform snapped off. They shattered against the diamond-hard ice beneath.

Paul keyed the controls and the craft came to life with a hum. Steam billowed from the back end as the frost and ice around the engine mountings melted free.

"This whole area is like a frozen graveyard, covered in all sorts of ships. Some are more intact than others," Paul explained. "We found these at a crash site not far from here."

There was a rail running around the skimmer at waist height where the piloting controls were, and at the very back. Abe leant against it as Paul brought the thrusters online, propelling them forward over the white landscape.

"Naturally, we explored the surrounding area shortly after arrival," Paul explained.

"You've probably noticed the old uniforms."

The wind tore at Abe's face, biting his skin. He turned his head out of the wind in order to catch his breath.

"Have you explored every wreck?" Abe shouted forward.

"More or less. Some were far too alien in origin to even begin to comprehend," Paul said.

Abe thought about that. He'd salvaged from a few outlandish ships in his time. Sometimes they hid real treasures. It was a question of knowing what you were looking at. Like telling fool's gold from the real deal.

"How many ships are there?" he shouted.

"Too many to count," Paul said. He pushed a lever forward and increased their speed.

As the white dunes rose and fell in smooth peaks and troughs, the skimmer maintained a mean distance from the surface at all times. Abe had ridden in anti-grav craft before, but never in a model so old and outdated. What they were riding was considered an antique.

"That reminds me. Where did I come down? Was it near?" Abe asked.

He thought of the 4Fava onboard. Of his weaponry. He felt naked without it nearby.

Paul pointed off to the left. Abe looked in that direction. In the very distance he saw the small grey peak of a lone mountain on the horizon.

"Just before that peak," Paul said. "We saw you enter the atmosphere and rushed to the scene as quick as we could."

Abe nodded silently, the cogs in his head beginning to creak into motion.

Paul pointed to a smooth hump on the landscape about two hundred yards away. Abe squinted against the rush of arctic air in his face. He saw an identical skimmer parked up in front of the hump of snow.

"There it is," Paul said.

He slowed their approach as they drew closer.

"What is it? A ship?"

"Yes. *Our* ship."

Abe didn't know if he meant it was *their* ship, the one they'd arrived in, or if he meant it was *their* ship, being the one that he was going to make it off the planet in. They stopped short of the hump of snow, and Abe saw the dull charcoal metal beneath showing through in places.

"Come on," Paul said, hopping down from the platform.

Abe did the same. They walked with heads lowered against the wind around the side of the hump, where they came to an exposed side of the ship jutting out from the ice and snow.

They were at the back end of the ship, and Abe recognised its configuration enough to see it was a Draxx transport. It was a kind he hadn't seen in years, not since his time in the army. They walked underneath the huge engine mounts, four funnels about ten feet across encrusted with monstrous icicles. There was an access hatch in the hull that had been left ajar. Paul pushed it open and stepped in. Abe followed behind.

It was dark inside apart from the emergency lighting that covered everything in a shadowy red hue. It was warm, almost humid. Abe smelled age and dust. Paul led him down a tight corridor.

Internally, the ship looked like any other. Ducting ran here and there, console panels along the walls, manually-operated levers and wheels jutted from random places. Most ships were designed and built to be completely functional and serve a purpose, to be workmanlike. Only the elite ships of the Union core worlds were built with any panache and grace. It was all you'd expect a Draxx ship to be.

When he thought about it, Abe had never seen a Draxx ship that wasn't crude and rough around the edges. They were a warrior race, their entire society and culture geared toward invasion and occupation. The vast Draxx Dominion's sole ambition was to spread like a reptilian cancer throughout the galaxy... that was how the Union spun it. Abe knew better. He'd seen worlds that the Draxx had ravaged and raped. And he'd seen the Union do the exact same thing, too. It was hard to tell the difference of one face from another.

He had seen what remained of the Dytarin System after the Terran Union had made use of its *Abolisher* weapon. They destroyed entire planets, reduced them to nothing more than scattered debris.

Because they were Draxx worlds, the action was justified. A victory.

Every chance he got, he stuck two fingers up at the Union and its Overmind-like control of the galaxy. One day, he was sure, a resistance would rise up against it.

That'll be the day, he thought.

"When we got in the ship, we didn't know any of the controls. Somehow we managed to get up into space, out of the combat zone. How we weren't shot down I don't know. *Luck.* We fled into deep space, without a direction or a clue where we were going," Paul said.

"Don't this tin can have a Jump Drive?" Abe asked.

"Yes and no. It doesn't work. We think that's why the Draxx left it there on Massa E Kym. Something happened to the Drive and they didn't have the time right there and then to do anything with it."

"Have you tried fixing it?"

"I'm not sure it's fixable," Paul said.

They turned a corner and entered a room. Abe took it to be the engineering quarter. It was on two tiers, connected by a ladder. Abe could hear noise from the upper level. Otherwise the ship was mostly silent. When you spent a lot of time in space you got to know the pulse of a starship. This one didn't have one. There was only the vaguest sense of energy coursing through it, like a very faint heartbeat.

"Before we entered this system we ran into a kind of thunderstorm in space. A nebula with massive electrical discharges going off inside. We couldn't avoid it. Have you ever seen anything like that before?"

"Yuh I have actually. In another place," Abe said, thinking back to his experience inside the Tiberius Corridor many months before. He nearly died, though he didn't tell Paul that.

"Well it was a rough ride, I can tell you. Shot us up pretty good," Paul said as he started to climb the ladder. Abe did the same, going up after him. "Our power was failing. When we exited the Rishi Drift we found ourselves here. We used the last of our power reserves to enter the atmosphere. It was either die here or die in space, and I thought if we had even the slimmest chance of survival down here we had to take it.

Unluckily for us, we hit the ground too hard and the ship was grounded."

Paul stood to one side as Abe climbed over the top of the ladder. There were two women on the upper decking on their hands and knees, fiddling with the underbelly of a control console. They worked together, sorting through the tangle of wires and circuitry that had spilled from it.

One had shoulder-length red hair tied back out of the way, the other short blonde hair. Both were sweaty and covered in grease and dirt.

"These are our resident miracle workers," Paul said.

The redhead got up off the floor and offered her hand. Abe shook it.

"I'm Laurie," she said.

"Abe," he said.

She jammed her thumb back at the other woman, who'd gone back to what she was doing.

"That's Court," Laurie said, "She's not being rude, but as you can see she's knee-deep in that mess."

"Making repairs," Abe stated, looking over at what Court was doing.

"You could call it that," Laurie said, "We've been slowly putting her back together... or trying to."

"Looks to be in good shape," Abe said, looking around. Though there was a lack of any real light he saw that the engineering section was ordered and tidy.

"Thanks," Laurie said.

"D'yuh think she'll get up in the air?" Abe asked.

"We're trying," she said, "We're almost done. Life support is back, everything else has been retraced and connected. We've done pretty much all we can. The problem is the power supply. Eighteen years in the ice has sucked the life out of it."

"Yuh..." Abe said.

Nearly two decades on this planet, he thought. He remembered the events of Massa E Kym as if they were only yesterday, when these men and women were left for dead on the war-torn surface of an alien world for no other reason than that the Union could grow replacements quickly and cheaply. It didn't feel like eighteen years had passed since then, though.

"She was in pretty bad shape. But over time we've managed to salvage enough parts to let us make the repairs she needs," Laurie said.

"I was telling Abe about the amount of ships there are around here," Paul cut in.

Laurie nodded. "There's loads. We've practically stripped them clean... apart from the really weird ones. There are some real alien designs out there. Those we haven't even touched."

Well that's the difference. They would've been the first ones I ripped open, Abe thought.

"I don't understand why you never fixed up any of the other ships around here," Abe remarked.

"They were all in too bad shape. Some were sitting here abandoned for decades. Believe it or not, the *Neberkenezer* was our best bet," Laurie said.

"Neberkenezer?"

"The name we gave her," Paul said.

Abe crossed his arms in front of his chest, the servos from his artificial limb whispered.

"So you've got things to sleep in, you've got clothes and supplies. You've got plenty of water around yuh. I get that. What I don't get is where the food's coming from. I didn't see yuh growing nothing in the caves, and it ain't like I've seen any hares hopping about the place," Abe said.

Laurie laughed.

"What's funny?" Abe asked with a smirk.

"Just the way you put that. If you want to know, then come this way and I'll show you where we get our food," Laurie said, going down the ladder.

Paul motioned for Abe to follow her.

As he mounted the ladder after her, Abe looked back at Court on her knees, attempting to make sense of the spaghetti spooled in front of her. She was separating the wires in her hands.

"Oy," Abe said. He could see she was flustered and confused by the mess in front of her.

She looked up.

"You're wasting your time sortin' through that mess."

She frowned. "Eh?"

"I said you're wasting your time, luv. I've got some experience. Trust me. Just rip all that out and bypass the system through the secondary capacitor. That'll fix yuh."

Although an alien ship, some key mechanisms were universal across the board and Abe knew it. Every system had its backup. There were always redundancies.

She looked down at the wires then back up with a relieved look on her face.

"Thanks!" she said.

"Yuh welcome," Abe said, going down the ladder.

15.

"*Shit?*" he asked.

"Well I prefer faeces, but as you like," Paul said.

Abe shook his head. On the bottom deck the matter processor was unlike any he'd seen before. They had them on most ships, and even the Draxx used them.

They were invaluable for long-term space travel.

"You're not fucking with me?" Abe asked.

Laurie shook her head, "Nope."

Abe looked the machine over. "Let's see if I'm right. This thing's meant to take matter like space dust, atmospheric by-product and the like, and re-constitute it into *food...*"

"Yes by breaking the matter down to the individual atoms and molecules and then processing them into whatever form you want them to take," Laurie said.

"But you don't have much of that stuff to feed into it. So you've been putting in..."

"Faeces" Paul said with a grin. "Or as you put it, *shit.*"

"I admit it sounds disgusting," Laurie said, "But it seemed the most logical way of recycling our waste. We were going to just dig a hole for it in the snow somewhere. And that would have been fine, but then when we realised what this was we saw an opportunity."

"It sounds worse than it is," Paul said, "We freeze our... *waste*... which as you can imagine isn't hard to do on this planet. Then it's simply a case of transporting it here a few times a week and putting it in."

"You turn *shit* into *food*..." Abe said incredulously.

Paul started to laugh. Laurie joined in. Abe couldn't help himself from laughing along with them, and he registered the shock on their faces at the sound of his deep hearty laughter. A heavy sound all at once enlightened and out of place.

"So what I ate earlier..."

Paul and Laurie nodded.

"I know it seems disgusting, but it's kept us going all this time. We'd have starved to death had we not had it," Laurie said, still laughing as she spoke.

"We tried feeding in ice from outside, but it seems to need something more substantial to work. And trust me, what you tried earlier is a lot more appetising than what we used to get out of it in the beginning. It's taken a bit of practice I can tell you," Paul said.

"It wasn't bad," Abe admitted.

"Now you know what we've been eating, I'll show you the bridge," Paul said as he led the way ahead. They went the length of the ship to the bow, Laurie behind Abe as he followed Paul.

"There ain't much left to say. It was originally a Draxx ship on the inside," Abe remarked.

"It's more or less the same tech," Laurie said.

"Yeah that and how tidy you've got it. I've been in Draxx ships in the past," he said as they passed neatly arranged data panels and sparkling clean ducts, "And I've never seen one looking like this inside."

The Draxx differed in appearance depending which homeworld they originated from. Regardless of how each different Draxx sect looked, they were nevertheless a united race. The Draxx Dominion spanned countless worlds across gigantic sections of space, but they answered to the same Queen. No living human had ever seen her, but she was known to exist, controlling the drones like bees in a hive. The Union had been hunting her since the war began.

"The smell was unbelievable," Laurie said. "And I tell you, it took us weeks to get rid of it."

"Rotten eggs," Abe said. He'd always known them to have a sulphurous odour.

"Yes that's it," Paul said as he opened the entrance to the bridge. It was no more than a long room with a helm console front and centre beneath a display screen, a station on the left for navigation and communication, and another on the opposite side for what looked like tactical operations. Purely functional, minimal and not unlike so many bridges he'd been on in the past.

"There's no seat for a Captain," Paul said. "So I take it when you're in charge you have to stand."

"Shows the crew your resilience," Laurie remarked.

"Never seen a Draxx sit, to tell the truth," Abe said looking around. "Don't know where they'd fit the tail. But then I don't think you'd be able to fit another chair in here anyhow."

"Probably right," Laurie agreed.

Even in the bridge there was only emergency lighting. "So you said about yuh power supply..." Abe said.

Laurie pulled up a chair at the navigation station and sat down. "Well, the core is still in good shape. But I can't have it at full cycle or we'd flood the surrounding area in radiation."

"Yuh," Abe said. He understood. If they switched it to full power, within days they'd irradiate everything for miles around. In space it didn't make a difference. But on a planet? Might as well set off a nuke.

"If we ever get out of here, I'm confident the core will fire up like it should and power the main engines just fine," Laurie said. "They have what? A hundred year lifespan before they have to be replaced?"

"Something like that," Abe said. That was true of human ships. Draxx ships differed, but he didn't voice this.

"The trouble is that the secondary energy banks are completely depleted. That means I have nothing to power any of the other systems, or to kickstart the core with. So, it's like I've got gas but no spark to light it with," she said. "When we went through that storm, it sapped most of it."

Abe thought for a moment. To even get in the air, the secondary banks were essential. Once they reached the upper layers of the atmosphere they'd switch to raw energy direct form the core. "How stuck is it?" he asked.

"What do you mean? How stuck is what?" Laurie asked, frowning.

"How stuck in the ice is this rust bucket? Could you clear it away from the hull?"

She shrugged. "We could. Might take a few days. But I don't know why you'd want to right now. Like I said we can't fire the core properly. Before too long she'd be iced over again."

Abe waved a hand at her. "Yuh. I know that. I'm not thick, pet. I'm asking for a reason. What's the weather like?"

"Good to fair. We shouldn't be due any real storms for a while yet. But when they hit, they *hit*," Paul said.

"Well, Laurie, if you can clear this ship I might be able to rig you a few solar arrays."

She sat forward in her chair. "What's that?"

"Old tech. You throw 'em on the hull, and they turn the sun's energy into electricity. Might take a while, but you can use them to recharge the secondary energy banks. It's a bit of a longshot but it's all I got until you can find another power source," Abe said.

Laurie looked at Paul. He nodded at her.

"Longshots are all we have," Paul said.

"I'll get on it first thing tomorrow," Laurie said, "And I'll take a list of whatever you need to make them. See what I can find."

"If you're sure you don't mind doing this..." Paul said to Abe.

"I'm stuck here with yuh. If you lot don't get off, then I don't get off," Abe said. "Might as well make myself useful."

Abe and Paul made to leave the bridge when Laurie spoke up behind them. They turned back around to face her. She was still in her chair. "There is one other thing," she said.

"Oh yeah... *this*," Paul said rolling his eyes.

"What?" Abe asked.

"We have no Jump Drive," she explained with a sigh, "So even if we do charge the energy banks, fire up the core and get into space, we can't really go anywhere, not without having to travel for months. What's left of it is scrap."

"Yuh. Paul mentioned this before. Have you had a go at fixing it?" Abe asked.

Laurie looked deflated. "Yep," she said.

Abe nodded and continued on out the door and back down the corridor.

Laurie shot Paul a *what was that?* look.

"One problem at a time," Abe called back.

16.

He rested in his tent when they got back to the camp, exhausted. He didn't sleep. Laying back on his bunk with his hands behind his head, he stared up at the ceiling as he considered his situation. He was without a ship, his only hope of getting off the surface was a rusted heap stuck in the ice with little more than a gnats chance of being space-worthy. He was in a cooperative mood, and it didn't sit easily with him. Being agreeable was not his modus operandi.

As much as his thoughts were concerned with whether or not he'd get off the planet, there was also the 4Fava sitting on his ship. An absolute fortune in narcotics. He had his weaponry in there too, and though he didn't feel that he needed to have it at hand, he preferred to have it nearby.

He sat up at the sound of someone entering the tent. It was Sara. "Hello again big boy."

She carried a tray with a bowl of piping hot food and a beaker of drink. She set the tray down on the end of the bed, and put the beaker on the little table by the side of the bed.

"Ta," Abe said.

"You're most welcome. How was the trip? I see it tired you out," she said.

"Uh... not so much," Abe lied. It had drained him.

"Paul took you to see the *Neberkenezer*, didn't he?" Sara asked. "Those girls have been working on it for ages."

Abe nodded. "They've done a good job. And I might be able to help them out with a few things."

"It sure would be nice to get that thing airborne and finally get off this planet," Sara said with a sigh.

"I can only imagine," Abe said.

He considered how the replicants growth was accelerated so that they could be sent into action as early as possible. From embryo to young adult in a handful of years. They didn't have a childhood. They existed to serve. If they hadn't made a run for it they would have suffered the same fate as every other replicant. Compared with how small their life experience had been, Abe had seen so much. Not only of the galaxy, but of life itself. Compared with him they were *innocent.*

"Well, anyway, I'd better be off," Sara said. "But I'll be back later. When you're finished just leave your tray on the side and I'll come grab it."

"Ta," Abe said again.

He watched her leave then pulled the tray closer. In the bowl was something resembling milky frog spawn. It smelled a lot better than it looked. He might've given it a miss ordinarily, but he was hungry again so he picked up the bowl and started slurping it down. It was sweet and creamy. He made a concerted effort not to think of the shit and piss it had been before being reprocessed.

"I'm glad to see you're eating," Paul said entering the tent unannounced.

Abe looked up at him and nodded in acknowledgement. "Friendly folks, ain't yuh," he remarked.

He hated people invading his personal space like that, but he was the guest of *their* domain and they *had* saved his life. All of the replicants lived together and shared resources, and he suspected that Paul's intrusion wasn't intentional, it had just become a habit. Still, if the situation were different he'd have sprung up from the bed and knocked Paul off his feet.

He didn't mind Sara entering unannounced though. As far as Abe was concerned, women could intrude any time.

"I know it wouldn't win any medals in a culinary contest, but it fills a hole. How are you finding it?" Paul asked him, sitting on the very edge of the bed.

Abe swallowed the last mouthful. "Tastes like shit," he said, cracking a grin.

For a split second Paul seemed taken aback but then he saw that Abe was joking. He chuckled. "Well, as you know..." Paul started.

Abe held up a hand. "Nah. Don't reminded me. It's not gone down yet. Aren't yuh eating too?"

"I've had mine. We *do* eat, you know... regardless of what they tell people about us. We do everything you do," Paul said.

"Eat, shit, and fornicate," Abe said.

Paul laughed. "Yeah. Something like that."

"Well like I told yuh, I don't listen to *them*. And there's a fair few just like me who'd like to see 'em brought down a peg or two. I've lived my life on the edge of the law. I've seen a lot of things. I've done a lot of things. I've seen how the Union conducts itself, mate, and I tell yuh... I'm not the only one who thinks the Galaxy's due a shake-up," Abe explained.

"You were in the army," Paul said to him.

Abe nodded. He was aware that he looked every bit a slow-witted, thuggish brute, and he spoke like it a lot of the time. But the years and the mileage had only served to sharpen him up. He was a cut-throat razor in a drawer full of spoons.

To him, his appearance and personality were like the different names he adopted. They were useful. In a life spent amongst the cold hard swirl of the stars, it was enough of a struggle to survive. In order to do that, in his experience, you had to employ certain talents.

"I did," Abe said, "And I was. But not for long."

"Is that when you lost your arm?" Paul asked.

Abe sniggered as he placed his empty bowl down on the tray. "No, that was a long time afterward," he said.

"I have to admit, you look like a man who's done a lot," Paul said.

Abe saw Paul's eyes take in the scars criss-crossing his face and the tattoos scrawled all over his head in an effort to disguise their markings.

"Yuh," Abe said as he ran his hand over his bald head. "Believe me, I've brought as much suffering as I've had to endure."

Abe had never spoken like that before, had never confessed of his true nature. He raced away from what he'd done. He acknowledged what he did and moved away from it at top speed. It was a grim truth that he had to accept. Every man had a shadow, but some fell darker than others.

There was silence between the two of them, and then Paul spoke up again.

"Earlier today you spoke of Massa E Kym, and you said you remember us being left behind, as good as dead. Humans seem to treat my kind with such ill-regard. It really doesn't bother you that you're here amongst replicants?" Paul asked.

Abe shook his head. "Replicants... *humans*... we all die the same, mate. You're survivors. I respect that. I've got no interest in a man who tucks his head between his legs when the going gets tough."

Paul looked down at his feet swinging off the edge of the bed. "We've been lucky that's all."

"By the looks of things, you've kept 'em together," Abe said.

Paul shrugged. "Yes I would say I'm their leader. But we don't have a direction. If we get off of here, I'm still not sure what we're going to do. We were the simple, heartless stooges of the Union. Doing what we were told without question or doubt. But that changed on the battlefield of Massa E Kym. We found *each other*, and then over the years here we've found *ourselves*. But still I feel as though we're..."

"Aimless," Abe said.

Paul nodded. "Yes that's it."

Abe knew how that felt all too well.

"There's a lot of replicants out there, just like it was eighteen years ago. Nothing's changed. Maybe a change is overdue," Abe said.

"Are you saying we should start some kind of... uprising?" Paul asked.

"Well, I saw you lot in action on Massa E Kym. I know you can fight," Abe said.

"What was your experience on Massa E Kym?" Paul asked.

Abe got up off the bed and walked back and forth. As he spoke, his mind rewound to all those years before.

"We were just kids. We'd all heard about Massa E Kym, but we didn't think we'd end up there. It-

17.

-is a curve of dark red, like blood, beneath the observation deck where the mission briefing is taking place. Abe is one of many fresh recruits standing to attention in the observation deck as the Fleet Commander enters, striding along in front of them. The deck is a long hall with large windows along one end and a massive screen on the opposite side. Fleet Commander DeMant approaches the podium in front of the screen.

"At ease," *she says and every troop, pilot, and mechanic assembled eases up a little.*

The lights in the room dim and the screen comes to life. DeMant's voice booms as she speaks.

"Boys and Girls, welcome to Massa E Kym. Or, as we call it, The Frontline."

Abe watches as the image of a planet appears on the giant screen - it is the planet over which they are orbiting.

The thick red thermosphere of Massa E Kym masks the planet-wide battlefield below, where Union and Draxx forces have been fighting for more than two years.

The world is now a torn, broken wasteland. They've all seen the pictures and the footage. They've read the reports of the action on the surface... and they've heard the chatter from those who have been there.

Command calls it the Front Line and DeMant calls it the Front Line. But the troops call it Hades. It's common knowledge that most who go down there don't come back. As their instructors tell them when pressed on what goes down on Massa E Kym: "Only life takers and heart breakers make it, so make sure you're both!"

After she details their mission, and what is expected of them, DeMant looks them all

136

*over as if she has nurtured them herself,
taken the soft balls of putty they started out
as and shaped them into roughened MEN
with her bare hands.*

*"You're this army's finest and I know
you'll make me proud," she says.*

*This is their first encounter with the
woman.*

*Next to Abe, Nicholson whispers
"Wanker" out the corner of his mouth. It
takes every ounce of Abe's reserve to resist
from hollering out loud.*

*"Remember your training, follow your
orders, and watch each other's backs,"
DeMant says.*

*"Bullshitting bitch..." Nicholson
whispers.*

*Abe starts laughing, quietly, looking
down hoping his superiors won't notice.*

*DeMant leans over the podium,
addressing them all as if she were lecturing
children. Her maternal smile masks the
intensity of her words.*

Abe wonders how many troops this woman has happily sent down to the surface with that same smile.

"Do me proud boys and girls, and go win back that planet!"

"Fuck yourself slut..." Nicholson says in a squeaky mouse voice.

Every man cheers, drowning out Abe's laughter.

It's the last memory he has of being blissfully go-lucky. It's the last time he will laugh like that, with such abandon. It's his last day as a boy. Massa E Kym makes a life-taker and a heart-breaker out of him.

After Massa E Kym, he is a man.

18.

"I was one of the few out of my squad who made it out of there," Abe said.

Paul considered what Abe had told him.

Massa E Kym had been a hell-hole. The Union had fought their campaign on the surface for longer than they'd ever fought anywhere else. The planet was strategically important, or so it seemed. Important enough to send millions of men, women, and replicants to their deaths to keep it.

"And the war continues?" Paul asked.

Abe nodded.

"Does the Union even remember why it's fighting them? I mean, *who* shot first at *who*?" Paul asked.

"It's just war mate. It's the nature of the beast. I discovered my talents on the battlefields like Massa E Kym. I learned how to kill a man. I owe something to the army in a way."

"Have you killed many people?" Paul asked.

"Yuh I have," Abe said instantly, his eyes locking with Paul's.

"And how does that make you feel?"

Abe lowered his head. "Like I don't deserve better than what I got," he said.

"You shouldn't talk like that," Paul said.

"Oh yeah? You don't know, mate. You don't have any idea what I've got myself into," Abe said.

"I can only imagine," Paul said.

Abe looked up, his eyes sore and red. "But you can't imagine. That's the problem. Nobody could possibly imagine the fucking horror I've seen. The hell I've brought on others. How do I feel? Like I shouldn't live. Yet I survive, anyway. I keep going, keep swimming so I don't sink and drown. I deserve what I got. Nothing."

"Every man deserves a chance to right his wrongs and make amends," Paul said softly.

Abe looked away. "Not me," he said, "I'll never change. Too long in the tooth."

He thought of the 4Fava on his ship. Even now he thought about how he would get to his ship to retrieve the drugs, and where he would hide it.

"Perhaps here, with us, you get a second chance," Paul said.

Abe took a deep breath, held it, exhaled slowly. He looked at Paul's honest face, his eyes bright and good and true. *Innocent.* He felt as though he were talking to a holy man. A priest.

It was like he was giving his confession. They didn't know what he was like. What he had done in the past. What he was capable of. Paul didn't understand how they were sheep with a wolf in their midst. It was liberating for Abe. He was under no threat here, he could let his guard down. He could relax for the first time in who knew how long. Maybe they didn't care about what he'd gotten up to. What if this was his second chance? His only shot at redemption for a lifetime of blood and fire?

"We won't judge you. We'll accept you for who and what you are. But the choice is yours. It seems to me you have an opportunity here to wipe the slate clean and start again. Become a new man," Paul said.

Abe looked up at the stretched fabric that was the roof of the tent. "Maybe," he said.

19.

When the night came Sara invited him on a walk to one of the other caves. She assured him that it was an easy stroll on the flat. Abe was secretly glad. They covered up in the same thick furs that he'd worn before, on the surface. Their footsteps clattered and echoed in the tunnel.

"That reminds me," Abe said as they walked alongside each other through the tunnel, their way lit by the same rods embedded into the ground in the main cave. "Where did you get the furs from?"

"This planet isn't totally devoid of life, as we discovered shortly after we crashed here," Sara explained. "Although they're not friendly animals. We call them Gundarks. Trust me, you wouldn't want to meet one out on your own. They're big."

"I can take care of myself," Abe said.

"So you keep saying. The thing is, I believe it too. A man doesn't look like you without being through a few scrapes," Said told him.

Abe said nothing.

"I didn't mean to insult you, I-" she started.

"It's all right. I know I'm not a pageant queen," Abe said.

"Yeah... No... I mean, I wasn't saying there's anything wrong with you..." Sara stammered.

Abe coughed quickly, stopping her dead. He pointed forward. "That the other cave?" he asked her.

Sara nodded, her face flushing red with embarrassment. "Yes," she said.

Suddenly she stopped. Abe took a few steps more then turned to face her.

"I'm sorry," she said. "I don't think there's anything wrong with you."

Abe snorted. "It's fine. I know what I look like. People used to call me Frankenstein," Abe said. He pointed to the rugged ruin of his face.

"Well, I mean what I said. I don't think there's anything wrong with you. Nothing worse than a man without feature," Sara said.

Abe dipped his head with a smirk, and then invited her silently with his hands to carry on walking, the air cleared.

"So why are we going here again? I thought you had nothing to do with the other caves," Abe said.

"There's something I want to show you. Something about us you need to understand. I like to come here every so often, just to check in," Sara explained.

Abe thought that a strange expression but didn't question it. They'd now reached the end of the tunnel. There were more of the lights arranged around the outer perimeter of the cave. Opposite the mouth of the tunnel he could see a wall of solid ice formed over the rock.

There was nothing else in the cave. They walked toward the ice, which looked like a frozen waterfall, smooth all over. Their breath trailed behind them, heavy and cold.

It wasn't until they got closer Abe understood why they were here. His sense of walking into a cathedral, or some place of communion was right. There were bodies in the ice. Frozen within it as if they'd fallen asleep stood up.

"Now you see," Sara said, her voice little more than a whisper.

"I do," Abe said.

"Many died over the years. I'm sure Paul said about it. So we made this their resting place. Somewhere we could visit them. Since the planet is more or less covered in ice we thought this was the best solution… we thought it was respectful."

Abe was stunned. "I don't want to sound like everyone else, but I never considered yuh people honoring their dead like this. Experiencing grief."

Sara looked up at the bodies, her eyes wet. "Of course we grieve. That's why I come here," she said.

"Which one is it?" Abe asked her.

Sara cried quietly, but it was controlled. Abe realized that she'd probably been coming here and crying like this for a long time.

"Jax, over there," Sara said. She pointed to a man suspended in the ice wall to their right. "Sometimes I pretend that he's just asleep. Once or twice I've caught myself believing I've seen his eyelids move. Of course I know it's a trick of the light. Just wishful thinking."

"Was he yuh partner?" Abe asked her.

Sara nodded, biting her lip. "He died a little while after arriving here. We loved each other. We had plans. We'd spend all night talking about what our future would be like when we got off the surface. But it wasn't to be. Even here on this lonely planet I thought I had someone. But I couldn't have it that way. The cold claimed him one day and took him from me. When we escaped from Massa E Kym I thought we were finally free. But then we crashed here. And now we're as much prisoners as we were before."

He didn't know why, but Abe felt suddenly compelled to hold her in some way. He reached across her shoulders and pulled her to him. She didn't resist. She hugged in close.

"I'm sorry," she said.

"Does it make the grief any less coming here?" he asked her.

"Sometimes. It's weird. Sometimes it just hits me, you know? I come in here, and I remember how much I miss him. I wish I could just melt the ice and set him free. But the only thing that would happen would be that the illusion would end," she said.

Abe held her in the semi-dark of the cave. The hollow sound of a *drip drip drip* echoed from somewhere in the shadows.

Sara had been a hardened doctor before, but all he saw next to him now was a frail, vulnerable *human being* with real emotions. She stepped away from him and wiped her eyes on her sleeve.

"Sorry-" she started but Abe held up a finger.

"Don't. Don't apologize again to me. You've shared something special, bringing me here. I'm glad you did," he said.

"Would you like to see something else? It might mean heading up to the surface for a bit, though," Sara said.

Abe didn't even have to think about it.

20.

The climb up to the surface was easier than before. Abe couldn't remember the last time he'd been on a planet where there was no artificial light pollution in the night sky. They stood outside the entrance to the tunnel. There was no wind, no sound save for the slight whisper of warm air coming up from the underground behind them. A massive kaleidoscope of stars and galaxies shone overhead. Ordinarily that alone would have been awe-inspiring, but the glittery-silver expanse of the Rishi Drift spread in a wide band among them took Abe's breath away.

"Pretty," Abe said.

"It is, isn't it? Nice to look at from down here. It's a volatile thing to travel through, though," Sara said.

Abe could see the electromagnetic storms erupting like fireworks within it. The Drift seemed to shimmer, also. He wondered if that shimmering effect was metallic dust within the cloud structure.

"Is this what yuh wanted to show me?"

"Yes. And just the night sky as it is. You know, sometimes I like to come out here and look up. Do you understand what I mean? I bet I sound silly."

Abe shook his head. "Nah, not at all pet."

He turned to look at her, illuminated by the starlight. In her eyes he caught the reflected phosphorescence of a million suns, burning icy white-hot. The light of infinity.

"It's nice to look at something beautiful once in a while," Abe said.

Sara took Abe's hand. She smiled. Abe managed a crooked smile of his own.

They both turned in time to see a shooting star disappear behind the shadow of a distant peak. Abe was reminded of his ship and what lay within its cargo hold. Now it seemed to him that his ship served as a reminder of the past, of his life up to the moment he'd crashed on the surface. Now, under the stars, he had his second chance… *if he chose to take it.*

"Paul said you were on Massa E Kym the same time as us. That you were in the army?" Sara asked him on their way back down.

"Yuh," Abe said.

There was silence for a few beats, and then Sara pressed him. "You don't have to tell me about it if you don't want to…" she said. "I don't want to force you."

"That's okay. I don't mind talking about it. I always remember the breakfast," Abe said, remembering that long-ago conflict. "Coffee, bacon, eggs, and-

21.

-dates. Bowls of dates. Abe sits chewing the sticky sweet flesh, spitting out the stone in the middle.

A hand falls on his shoulder. It's Nicholson.

"Come on fucker! We gotta move out!" he yells in his ear.

"Hey! For fuck sake, I'm eating!" Abe snaps back.

Abe gets up, shoveling a handful of the fruit into his mouth before taking after Nicholson. The rest of the mess is clearing out, everyone receiving their individual orders. The assault on Massa E Kym is resuming, with the intention of striking at multiple targets on the planet's surface.

Abe and Nicholson arrive at the small briefing room just in time. Their commander eyes them with distaste as they take their seats.

"Our objective is the Gamma base, sector six," he says, turning to a visual display of the terrain on the surface. The long oblong compound of the base is highlighted in luminous yellow.

"You are to re-take it with any and all force at your disposal. We do not observe the rules of war here, gentlemen. Take that base back out of Draxx hands... at all costs. Any questions?"

He looks them all over, satisfied they fully understand their orders. He dismisses them.

"Good luck people," he says as they file out of the briefing room and make tracks for the equipment lockers.

Abe throws on his light armour, pulls out his battle helmet with BEAST stenciled across it. Nicholson hands him a heavy type-nine laser cannon and a lightweight *proton musket which he slips into his sidearm holster.*

"Any more sonic grenades in there?" Abe asks.

Nicholson looks inside the locker, then checks the next one over.

"Nah, the fucking dizzies must've rinsed 'em mate," he says.

Abe spits on the floor. "Fuck!"

A klaxon sounds and the lights in the room change to a heavy, pulsating red.

"Come on. We better move," Nicholson says, ruffling Abe's short black hair and running out into the corridor.

Abe follows, slapping on his helmet as he runs, cursing DZ Company for taking the best of the ammo.

22.

The transport detaches from the belly of the ship and the pilot immediately fires the thrusters, propelling them down into the thick hellish red haze of Massa E Kym. The transport bucks and jitters against the atmosphere, part of an invading swarm.

"Not shitting yourself are ya?" Nicholson asks, elbowing him in the ribs.

There's about twenty of them crammed into the transport but none of them look in his direction. They're all concentrating on their own fear. Their apprehension in deploying to the battlefield.

He himself feels cool and collected, in a way that worries him more than if he were writhing in his seat with panic. He rides into battle breathing steady.

And Nicholson bouncing up and down, excitable? That only means he's as scared as he's ever been.

"Thirty seconds!" the pilot shouts from the front. There are no windows inside the transport. It's like riding a tin coffin from orbit.

"Here we go," Nicholson says, strapping on his helmet.

"Yuh," Abe says, simply, his tightly balled fists in his lap.

The transport is buffeted by enemy fire, and the pilot does a good job of swerving around the worst of it as they make their rapid descent. Within minutes they're slowing to land at the designated co-ordinates, along with the other transports. The ship hits the ground hard. The pressure equalizers fire with a hiss, and the rear doors burst open. The men file outside into the burnt orange fog that perpetually shrouds the planet.

Abe looks up briefly as he steps out of the transport, seeing the shadows of the other transports descending through the haze around them. Bright bursts of Draxx fire light the sky like bolts of thunder.

"Move, move, move!" their group commander yells, leading them forward. Abe sprints with the other men, glancing down at his cannon for the tenth time to check that it's fully armed. Movement to his left makes him look in time to see the form of a Draxx charging their flank. It's a Draxx warlock. Abe lifts his cannon quickly, firing at it without even thinking. The Draxx is blown backwards separating at the mid-section as it flies through the air. The other men start firing left and right, attacked by more warlocks.

"Fire at will! Maintain formation!" their commander yells from the front, pushing ahead as his men open fire behind him.

"Nicholson, Three O'Clock!" Abe shouts as a cluster of warlocks charge their right. Nicholson fires at them. Abe levels his

cannon at one, fires. The Draxx's head is blown away and yet the body still runs before falling to the dirt.

"We're coming up on it. Hold tight."

Above them Union starfighters engage Draxx ships. Explosions shatter the air.

The shadow of the Gamma base compound emerges up ahead. Their commander spins about, still running backwards, points at Abe.

"Beast, light the trail!" he orders.

"Sir!" Abe falls back as the others run on ahead, and unclips a sonic grenade. He twists the top of it around, pushes the clip forward and then throws it over his shoulder. He runs as fast as he can, and seconds later the area they'd just run through is decimated with a massive sonic explosion. If there are any more warlocks coming in from behind, the explosion obliterates them.

There's a huge thunderclap from up ahead, and when he catches up with the *others they've already breached the wall of the base and are piling inside. Their commander puts two men on point, and huddles with the rest.*

"This is a flush and clear, right? Every moving thing in this building that doesn't have five fingers and toes gets swatted. The reppies are already in here cutting a swathe through these green skin motherfuckers. We go in behind and pick up the flack."

He looks from one man to the other. "Do you get me!?" he shouts at them.

"YES SIR!" they shout back in unison.

"Good. Rolo, Tango, and Beaks, you take the east side. Flush 'em out. Beast, Nicholson, Rabbit and Fang... you take the west," he orders them. "I want carnage, gentlemen!"

He stands back from them. "Move! Move! MOVE!"

Abe, Nicholson, Rabbit and Fang go left along a tunnel. The inside of the base is dark, with minimal emergency lighting that fades in and out due to dying power. They pad forward, guns held in front, their eyes darting left and right, searching the shadows for movement.

Abe feels his pulse at the back of his eyeballs, thrumming. A trickle of sweat runs beneath his vest and his combat gear and down his back.

The sound of the others in their team falls to the distance as they travel along the corridor.

"Movement," Rabbit whispers from the corner of his mouth. They all stop and get low, watching the tunnel.

At first Abe doesn't see it. But seconds later the dark is disturbed like a hand swirling water. Six Draxx foot-soldiers step forward, out of the shadows and raise their weapons at the sight of the Union soldiers hunkered down in front of them.

Fang springs up, jabbing his cannon at the face of the lead Draxx and firing at the same time. Nicholson lifts his weapon where he is, hunkered down on the floor, and fires a spread at them whilst Abe and Rabbit rise up and press forward, firing into them. The Draxx soldiers are blown left and right, legs and arms pirouetting through the air in spurts of reptilian gunge.

They cease firing and listen for the sound of more Draxx coming their way.

"Fall back!" Nicholson snaps at them, and they instinctively run back a few paces. They watch as he removes a grenade and primes it. He tosses it forward down the tunnel.

"Gonna be a snake buffet," Rabbit sniggers next to Abe.

Nicholson hustles back to them, shooting Abe a quick look. "He said flush 'em out, didn't he?" he says with a grin.

"Well, yeah-" Abe says and then turns his head at the sound of something rattling along the floor toward them. Before he sees it properly, or gets the words out of his

mouth, Fang screams "GRENAAAAAAADE!!!!!!"

They run as fast as they can. The mouth of hell opens behind them, an explosive roar. Hot breath rushes Abe off of his feet and sends him hurtling through the air. He crashes to the floor, skidding along on his front.

"Urgh," he groans as he lifts himself up and turns over.

He can't see his cannon anywhere. To his right he sees Fang lying still on the ground, his lower half blown away. Next to Fang lies Nicholson's crumpled form. The stencil of an ace card still visible on his helmet. Abe hears Draxx laughter, a terrible, screeching sound. They are rushing the tunnel and headed his way. Bits of the wall are alight, the corridor flickering.

Abe sits up. His head whirls. He tries to stand but his legs are jelly. Searching the floor he still can't see his cannon. The Draxx are coming.

Abe feels his side for his musket. He removes it from his belt and arms it. His vision blurs so he closes one eye, lifts the musket in front of him, and aims. The first Draxx runs around the corner and Abe waits until he has a clear shot before firing. Proton rounds tear holes straight through the reptilian body, and it staggers to the floor. Jets of blood spurt everywhere. Two more barrel towards him and he fires again. From his low position they can't see clearly where the shots come from, and not before the proton bolts take them down.

The two Draxx trip over each other and crash against a wall. He drags himself toward Nicholson. Abes's legs still refuse to work.

He turns Nicholson over. The entire front of the soldier's torso is laid open like the exposed flesh of an orange. Floods of bodily fluids cover the floor.

"Hey," Abe says as Nicholson's eyes open and he becomes aware that Abe is there.

"... Abe..."

"What about Rabbit?" Abe asks Nicholson. Abe's eyes glance around but see no sign of Rabbit anywhere.

"I think he got the grenade first, buddy," Nicholson whispers.

More movement comes their way. Abe lifts his musket and fires at two more Draxx. One falls immediately, the other takes cover at the corner and starts firing back. Abe shrinks away from the randomly placed discharges that erupt around him. They clang off of walls and floor.

"Just go," Nicholson says. Blood gushes from his mouth and his eyes roll in his head.

Abe's eyes fill with tears. He bites them back. Not now. Not here.

"I'm not leaving you behind," Abe says. He crouches against incoming Draxx fire.

Nicholson reaches up and grabs him by the top of his vest.

"I said GO."

Rage. Pure, unadulterated rage.

"NEVER!" he screams. His heart pounds inside his chest. Adrenaline surges. He rises, musket raised, and fires at the nearest Draxx foot-soldier. He stomps forward firing without pause.

He charges. The Draxx raises its weapon but Abe blows its head clean off before it pulls the trigger.

Abe races down the corridor firing as he runs. The red mist of the planet wraps itself around his brain like the many-tentacled roots of a virulent weed.

He feels nothing but fury, and every part the beast of his namesake. Draxx appear in front of him but he executes them without pause, his teeth clenched, their cold blood splashed across his face. He doesn't wait for their bodies to fall. He doesn't slow. He runs through the base, killing at near point-blank range.

He turns a corner, ready to fire. A human face, gaping in horror stands before him, frozen. She raises her hands and screams, "Whoa! Stop!"

He rests with his hands on his knees, head down, panting. How many has he killed? The musket is suddenly too hot in his hands, and he drops it to the floor.

The female soldier glances down at the spent weapon and then rests a hand on his shoulder.

"Easy soldier," she says, "You've nearly burnt that weapon out. I've never seen one with smoke coming out of it before."

He stands, his head rushing. Abe swallows to clear it.

The woman is young, but she looks experienced. Then he notices the uniform. It is dark blue; a replicant. There are more replicants behind her, standing point outside the door to a room.

"We've taken the base," she says.

She looks him over, at the blood on his face, at the streams of sweat and tears that have mixed into one on their way down his face.

"And you've taken a few of them I see."

Abe swallows.

"The others were killed. I lost my weapon. I took out as many as I could..."

She holds up a hand to him and turns to the side, listening to the comm feed in her ear.

She looks to the others.

"Everyone, our orders are to escort any remaining friendlies to evac," she says.

They file out, running. She puts her hand behind him and makes Abe run with her.

"Where are we going? Is the base secure?" Abe asks.

"Forget the base. They're calling it all off. We've gotta get you to the evac point, stat."

"I don't understand..." Abe manages as he is led outside through an opening in the wall of the base. He looks up at the sky in time to see a huge shape descend through the gloom. An awesome rumble sounds as the atmosphere parts to allow the immense battleship to land. The ground shakes as the ship continues toward the surface.

"What the fuck...?" he gasps, still being led with the female soldier's hand at his back, guiding him forward.

"Command says the Draxx have retaken the planet. That's probably a dreadnought," she says.

They mount a hill and hit the evac point which overlooks the base. A transport sits ready, half-filled with wounded men and women from different companies. The female officer shoves Abe aboard, and he hears the engines whine.

He holds out his hand for her, but she takes a step back.

"Not my orders," she says. Her men stand behind her, weapons at the ready.

"What?" Abe asks her, and then is sent stumbling backwards into a seat as the transport lifts off the ground and tilts its nose into the air, moving upwards. The hatchway closes and he stumbles out of his seat, pressing his face against the glass. The tortured terrain falls away and they are enveloped by the red cloud cover.

"We can't leave them behind!" he yells, turning to look at everyone else aboard.

A commanding officer comes forward and lends a comforting a hand to the back of his neck.

"No can do, son, orders are for the reppies to stay behind."

"Why?" Abe asks.

"Don't matter," the officer says.

Abe stands up, angry. "Yeah it does, fucker!" he yells, shoving him in the chest. Another soldier gets up and rushes over, pushing Abe back.

"Easy!"

The commanding officer, PETERS it says on his right breast pocket, grins.

"Don't get uppity over a few fucking reppies, son. You got out alive. Be thankful they're staying behind so that you can get out."

Abe's fists fall to his sides, defeated.

"It shouldn't be like this. We shouldn't leave them," he says.

"They don't matter," Peters says, grinning. "They're just cannon fodder. Get used to it."

23.

"I think I've blocked out what I saw there," Sara said with a shudder.

Abe nodded. "I was changed after that. I wasn't a boy no more."

"So that explains your affinity towards us," Sara said as they neared Abe's hospital tent. "Why you have no prejudice."

"Yuh."

She thumbed at the tent, changed the subject. Abe's recounting of his experience on Massa E Kym had been raw and honest and had brought back a few memories Sara would have prefered to leave buried.

"By the way, I might be needing this tent back soon," she said. "I've got a patient who's going to need it."

Abe's eyebrows rose. "Oh?"

Sara crossed her arms. "Yeah, she's about thirty-eight weeks now I think. Her name's Abby."

It took a second for this information to register with Abe, but when it did he couldn't keep the surprise off of his face. "One of you got pregnant?"

"Yes. Amazing isn't it? I know, we're not meant to be able to procreate. But what can you do? They've been trying a long time," Sara said, pleased.

Abe shook his head. "That's what we were always told. That it couldn't happen. I thought the quacks manipulated your genome to stop it?"

"Well, evidently not enough," Sara said.

Abe knew from experience that when replicants were used in the sex trade, one of the advantages was that firstly they couldn't get pregnant, and secondly sexually transmitted diseases had no effect. They didn't act as a carrier for them, either. Of course some men still paid for the services of *proper* humans, but the replicants were doing a good job of putting them out of business.

There was a an awkward silence before Abe reached out with his robotic arm, rested it on her shoulder. "Thanks for spending time with me tonight," he said awkwardly.

She reached up, laid her hand over his, squeezed it. She looked happy. Abe wondered if he had ever been guilty of making a woman happy before. God knew he'd been guilty of everything else over the years.

"Nice to have someone to spend time with for once," she said with a smile.

He bid her goodnight then retired inside his tent, now conscious that it might not remain his for long. It didn't take him long to fall to sleep, and for once he slept well. There were no dreams. Only the darkness of his mind, and the silence of eternity offered by the vacuum of unconsciousness. A good rest.

In the morning he made a promise to himself that his help would not stop with getting them off the planet's surface. He'd help them afterwards too, if he could.

Remembering Massa E Kym, and the young kid he'd been, made him think about the amount of time he'd spent living a selfish, singular life. He was guilty of unthinkable things, and none of that had ever bothered him before... but it did now.

Abe felt a grim determination to see to it that every replicant had the chance and choice of freedom, whether the Union liked it or not. He woke certain that only in revolution – *in freeing the millions of replicants enslaved by the Union across the Galaxy* – would he find any kind of atonement for the way he'd gone about his life. There was redemption to be found. Amongst the stars, and the many battlefields between. He just had to embrace it.

24.

The Union Battleship 'Attila' T.U.6641

Admiral Royce surveyed the readouts at the navigation station with his hands clasped tightly behind his back. He nodded as the young officer explained the various results displayed on the large flat panels. Three months of combing the galaxy for the small smuggling ship that had slipped from his grasp finally paid off.

"And you're certain?" he asked him.

Ensign Nimmera swallowed. Royce knew that he made the younger men nervous. They had good reason.

"Yes sir, of all the probes dispatched throughout the galaxy, this was the only one to return with any results," Nimmera said.

As soon as he learned that the little ship that had avoided capture was that of the galaxy's most wanted man, Royce ordered a galaxy-wide search. They dispatched automated probes to every uninhabited planet on the charts, an effort that had thus far gone without success. Until now.

Royce leaned forward and read from the screen. "The Rishi Drift..." he said. He hadn't heard of it. A Union survey vessel had marked its position and name it centuries before.

"Yes Admiral. It's a debris field that surrounds the whole system. Nebulous clouds, some unstable matter and debris. Quite dangerous to travel through," Nimmera said.

"That is of no concern, Ensign. Not for the Union's flagship. And the planet lies beyond that barrier?"

Nimmera nodded.

Royce slapped him on the shoulder. "Good work, young man. Keep it up."

Several officers stood to attention and saluted as Royce turned on his heels and exited the bridge. He strode to his private ante room where someone waited for him in the shadow of the viewport. The doors slid shut behind him.

"We've found him," Royce said.

The figure stood up, smiling. *She has a lovely mouth*, Royce thought. He'd gotten to know Neary very well during their search for The Tattooed Man. It was a name the press had given the galaxy's most wanted man, and Royce thought it apt.

She drew close to him, slid her hands round his waist. He saw she still wore the same silky nightgown from earlier that morning.

She kissed his neck, and he bore it... but he did not reciprocate.

"I'm so proud of you," she whispered in his ear.

He took a step back and held her at length. Confusion washed over her face.

"What's wrong? Aren't you pleased?" she asked.

Royce maintained eye contact with her as he spoke. "Our arrangement is over from here on in. I'll need you to remove whatever *things* you have lying about in here," he said coldly.

"But... but... I thought..." she stammered.

"You were mistaken," Royce said.

He glanced down at his watch, an old timepiece from Earth's history. It was a rare trinket to find in such modern times but he liked it. It served as a reminder of where he came from, that of all opponents to be found in the universe time was the deadliest.

"You can't do this to me. Without me, you wouldn't have found him. I helped you. What's going to happen to me?" Neary said as she backed away from him.

Royce sighed with irritation. "I don't have time for this. I'll have some of my men help you *remove* yourself."

He turned and left. She screamed hysterically behind him. The closing doors muted her voice.

Two officers arrived, just as he had arranged.

"Be quick and clean. I don't want any mess on the carpet," he told them.

They nodded in the affirmative and saluted him as he turned and left.

Half an hour later Neary's body was jettisoned into the vacuum of space. A short while after that, Admiral Royce ordered the Attila to make the Jump to light speed.

25.

"Before we get there, I ain't been totally honest with yuh mate," Abe said.

Paul piloted them over the white dunes toward what was left of Abe's ship. Abe stood with his head lowered against the bitter rush of the wind.

Paul looked up. "Oh?"

"I was transporting drugs before I ended up here. Someone I used to know set me up, and before I knew it I had a Union ship on my back. I made the Jump just as a missile hit my back end, and that's what knocked me here. That's why I crashed."

Paul shrugged. "Why is that a problem?"

Abe was thrown. He'd rehearsed this conversation over and over in his head before setting out, and he was not a man to worry about how he would be received. But the replicants had been good to him, and they were all in the same boat. They'd all been defecated on from above.

"Well, I thought it just might..." Abe started.

"Look Abe, your business is your business. We all know you're obviously not a saint. You've got up to a few things in your time. But that's none of our concern. All that matters is that you're here now, with us. And you're stuck here, with us," Paul said.

Abe sighed. "Yuh all surprise me."

"Why?" Paul asked him.

"Because you're good. You're innocent, I 'spose. Yuh don't have any preconceived beliefs or prejudices. No moral high-grounds. The only thing burdening yuh all is what the Union did to yuh," Abe explained.

"I guess you're right there," Paul said. He slowed the platform and swung it around to the left. Abe saw the battered hulk of his ship encrusted in thick ice. It had only been a few weeks. It was obvious that the ship would soon be consumed by the frosted skin of the planet, like a scab over a cut.

Paul stopped short of the ship and the two of them hopped down.

"Here, use this," Paul said, tossing Abe a handheld device that Abe recognised as a flame thrower.

"Cheers," Abe said with a grin. "Haven't played around with one of these in a long time!"

He aimed at his ship and pulled the trigger. A thick belt of billowing flame engulfed the starboard side. The ice melted away. Steam rose from the point of contact. In short order he cleared enough of the ice to allow him access to the cargo hatch.

He squatted down as he pulled the contents out onto the ice with Paul watching over his shoulder.

"Doesn't seem a lot there," Paul said.

Abe laughed. "It don't mate. But when you know how much it's worth, you realise you don't need a lot. This little stash is worth a mint."

"And those?" Paul asked, pointing to several metal cases Abe set next to the packages of 4Fava.

Abe patted one of the cases. "These are mine. Tools of the job, you could say."

After securing the contents of the cargo hold onto the back end of the platform, Abe went to the cockpit and dangled inside from above. He worked at the flight console with his big, thick hands, wiggling free a black box. He returned to the platform with it, sparing his old ship one last glance as Paul fired up the engine and circled about.

"What is that?" Paul asked.

Abe lifted the black box with a grin. "A little something that might come in handy," he said.

Paul nodded appreciatively and pointed the platform back in the direction of the camp. He ramped up the speed. The craft rose and fell with the dips in the snow.

Abe looked around the smooth, monotonous landscape. The sun glared off the white and he squinted against it. Such a barren planet, a frozen wasteland. And yet they had survived here. Endurance. He had a great respect for people who could endure against all odds.

He had wanted so strongly to get to his ship and lay his hands on the 4Fava. And now he wasn't entirely sure what he would do with it. There was a fortune in narcotics at Paul's feet, and Abe wondered whether he could use it somehow to help them.

Off to the east there was a flash of light against a low rise on the horizon. Abe lifted a hand to his brow and squinted. The sun caught whatever it was again.

"Eh! What's that then?" Abe said.

Paul looked in the same direction. After a few beats he angled the craft towards it. "Let's go and have a look," he said.

The alien ship was nose down in the thick ice, the silver hull plating on both sides fractured and torn from impact. Abe examined the rear engine cluster with his hand shielding his eyes from the sun's glare. He saw fire damage on two of them.

"Another victim of this planet," Paul said beside him.

Abe grunted. He noted the scorch marks above the engine mounts, from the weapons of an enemy vessel he guessed.

"I've not seen this before," Paul said.

"That don't surprise me, mate. The snow and ice probably contracts and flexes all the time. It hides and reveals whatever's under it," Abe said. He walked towards the side of the hull. Where two of the large chrome tiles of the outer hull met, there was a larger gap there than anywhere else. He ran his hand over it, feeling several bumps in one area.

Holding the palm of his hand against it, something within the ship registered life.

Seconds later the gap in the hull opened like a doorway.

Paul took several steps back in surprise.

"Don't worry, Paul," Abe said. He leaned into the hatchway and sniffed the air coming from the ship. "Air's bad. She's been here a long time, my friend."

"Will you need a re-breather? I have one stored in the back," Paul asked.

Paul unfastened a small metal case from one of the railings on the platform. He opened it and removed a re-breather unit.

"You not coming?" Abe asked as he took the unit from him.

Paul shook his head. "I only have the one," he said.

Abe stuck it into his mouth. The twin canisters attached to the sides of the mouthpiece would give him an hour of breathable air.

Paul un-clipped a torch from his belt and handed it to Abe, who nodded in thanks.

Without further ado Abe ducked his head into the ship then stepped inside. The darkness of the ship's interior swallowed him whole.

Abe emerged twenty minutes later to find Paul pacing on the ice.

"Thank goodness," he said. "I was starting to worry."

Abe removed the re-breather and handed it back to him. Under one arm he had a large circular device, like a big bell jar. Metal contacts at the top and bottom of a ball of clear glass.

"What was it like inside?" Paul asked him.

Abe walked to the platform, setting the device down on it. "Alien," he said.

"Were there any bodies?" Paul asked.

Abe climbed onto the platform. He was so much stronger now than when Paul had showed him the *Neberkenezer*.

"A few. But they were old. Like I said, this ship's been here a while. Whoever they were, they won't be playing in a band any time soon."

Paul climbed up and glanced back at the alien vessel. The doorway in the hull closed itself. He started up the platform and headed for home.

"Tough going in there," Abe said.

"Really?" Paul asked.

"Well yuh, the ship's arse end up ain't it? It was easy getting to the front. It's when I had to get back up to the back end I had trouble."

"Ah. I see," Paul said. "We found many such vessels in the past. Some of them we salvaged from, some of them were far too alien to even consider taking from. So anyway, what was that you found?"

"Something that might make your two beautiful grease monkeys very happy," Abe said.

"Oh?" Paul's eyebrows rose in surprise.

Abe went to the front of the platform and put his arm around Paul, grinning in the way psychotic career criminals do when something's gone their way.

"Our ticket outta here."

26.

All of the replicants gathered in the main cave. Abe watched from the side as Paul explained the plan to them. The item Abe had pulled from the alien craft was a foreign version of a power core. It still had a lot of life left in it. More than enough for the *Neberkenezer* to escape the grasp of the planet.

Laurie and Court jumped up and down with excitement when they ran an analysis of it and detected the steady thrum of power at its centre. A team now worked to free the ship from the snow and ice that held it captive.

"... and once we get out into space, our friend Abe has offered to help us find our way," Paul said with a nod in Abe's direction. "And that is something we all need to give serious thought to."

There were murmurs from the other replicants. One of them stepped forward, a black man with a bald head. Abe had heard someone call him by the name of Stape.

Stape looked around. "And just what are we going to do? What's the plan?" he asked Paul.

"Well there's no real plan. Sounds crazy when you consider how long all of us have been stuck here. But I do have one notion. We need to find a home. I'm not sure how that's going to happen, or where we'll go..."

"Anywhere there's no Union!" Stape said to a few cheers.

Paul held up his hands. "It goes without saying. Wherever we set ourselves to pasture, it needs to be somewhere we can live. Build homes, farm the land, write, sing... *make babies*," Paul said with a smile.

Abe watched as another replicant came forward, as if on cue. Abby held her pregnant stomach. Straight away Abe spotted the wet running down the insides of her legs. Her face was tight and frightened.

"How about we start with this little one," she said.

Sara came from nowhere. She shot a look at Abe as she rushed to Abby's side.

"Quick."

Abe walked over and without a second's hesitation picked Abby up in his arms and carried her to his tent with Sara in tow. He'd have to find somewhere else to sleep.

27.

He stayed out on the *Neberkenezer* by himself. The ship had a few individual quarters and a long sleeping area with twenty separate racks. It was quiet, but in the familiar way that all starships are when they are idle. That is, not completely quiet. He listened to the gentle *tick tick tick* of machinery. Life support systems kept the ship's air clean and fresh, whilst maintaining a moderate temperature.

Abby had brought a perfectly healthy baby girl into the world. Whatever world this was, anyway. From what Sara had told him of the child, the genetic trait of dual-coloured eyes was not apparent. Her eyes were hazel brown. It occurred to Abe on the ride out to the *Neberkenezer* that the child was a new iteration of human being. A third generation human. He wondered what the implications of that would be.

Laurie and Court asked him if he was comfortable staying there by himself. Even they returned to camp every night to be with the others. He just laughed. He wasn't a man who got afraid of the dark. Abe liked to think the dark was afraid of *him*.

He put himself to use and spent each waking minute doing what he could to hurry the Neberkenezer along and make her space-worthy. The girls had done excellent work, and he admired their craftsmanship. The old ship was nearly ready. However, many of the back-up systems needed work, and the girls had incorporated a lot of old Union components into the Draxx technology. All of it needed to be tested, to be sure it wouldn't fail them once they reached space. If any of it was going to throw a wobbler, then better to do it whilst they were grounded. Not thousands of miles into space.

He was on his knees beneath a console, plugging the main feeds into a diagnostic device. He sipped a cup of hot soup as he went about his business. Abe wasn't sure what time it was, but the others were no doubt asleep by now.

Abe heard a noise behind him, in the corridor. He slid out and grabbed a wrench. They were alone here, he was sure of it. But what if that wasn't the case? What if another ship had landed and they were checking the *Neberkenezer* out? What if it was one of the Gundarks Sara told him about? Anyone other than a replicant wandering through the ship was going to get a pretty big surprise when they found Abe pouncing out on them.

"Abe?"

He lowered the wrench when he heard Sara's voice.

"In here," he yelled.

She turned the corner. "Ah there you are," she said.

"Hi yuh," he said with a smile.

"I wasn't sure if you'd be asleep or not," she said.

Abe dismissed it. "Why aren't you in bed?"

Sara shrugged. "Couldn't sleep."

Abe never had any trouble sleeping. He believed every man had a ghost or two he carried with him, but his own never bothered him. He didn't sleep much out of habit. But when he did, he slept like a baby.

"So how come yuh didn't just fetch yourself a drink and go back to bed?"

Sara's eyes locked with his, and they held. "I wanted to see you," she said.

"Why?"

Sara stepped forward, took his hands into her own. "Because I've been thinking about you."

"Listen," Abe said. Sara pushed a finger up against his lips.

"Stop. I'm a big girl. I know what I'm doing," she said. "The truth is, I couldn't sleep because of what you said."

Abe chuckled. "Have I got myself into trouble?"

"No. Nothing like that. Look, do you remember when I asked you about the name you were calling out? When you were in and out of it?"

Abe nodded.

"What's the real story?" she asked, her eyes bright.

Abe took a step back, turned away from her. He ran his hands across his face.

"You don't want to talk about it," Sara said.

"No it's not that..." Abe said.

There was a long silence. He turned back around. "I was hiding out on a ship. For a few months, you know. Keep my head down. Stay out of trouble. Wait for the heat to cool. But something happened. I was down in engineering and-"

28.

-he knew something was up when he heard the sound of another ship clamping itself to their side.

Abe was on his hands and knees in the engine room cleaning the proton filter plates when he felt the rumble of what could only be a gravity well drawing close to the ship. He wondered if it was an asteroid skimming past them. But then he heard the unmistakable scrape of metal on metal and a loud crash.

He stood and listened, forgetting about the proton plates. By the sound of it they were on the starboard side of the Royale. The security seals on the airlock would not open easily for them, whoever they were, but they could cut through in no time.

If they were Draxx, they would be inside the ship in moments. If it was an attack by pirates or mercenaries, then it depended on their equipment. Some melted the seals, some blasted them clean off... and some simply breached the ship itself by drilling through the outer shell. That was a much less common method of gaining access, though, as you risked hitting major ductwork and blowing both ships. But if you were that desperate to get inside you'd take that risk. Abe knew that.

He wondered if he should go up to the command centre and offer his assistance to the rest of the crew, or remain in the engine room and see who their visitors were before taking action.

Fuck 'em I'll wait, *he thought.*

He took the heavy metal rod he'd been using to clean the filter plates and smashed the lighting panel. The engine room plunged into complete darkness. He didn't want intruders being able to flick the light back on. Abe sat and waited.

29.

Frankenstein was their nickname for him, and he supposed he really did look a bit like the eponymous Monster. In fact he quite liked it. None of them could have guessed at his real name. They took the moniker he'd given them – simply 'Frank' and nothing else – as gospel.

If only the rest of the crew knew where he had been over the years, what he'd done, they wouldn't have taunted him the way they did. The crew were all from Earth – the very core world around which the whole of the Terran Union radiated - and they were all more refined, a far better breed. They were handsome people despite their inherently disgusting natures, clean and well-groomed.

There was a distinct class divide between those born on Earth and the people of the outer colonies who were decades behind the advancements of the rest of the Union. As you moved further and further away from the core worlds, the standards of living and society deteriorated. Some of the more backwater worlds were at least a century behind others simply due to their distance from the rest of Galactic civilisation.

Abe's duties on-board consisted of working in the engine room and maintaining anything mechanical. This meant that he was almost always dirty and covered in grease and sweat from his labors. The others mocked him, called him names because of it. He also carried out general janitorial duties and the crew wasted no time in telling him when one of the toilets was broken or blocked-up.

Normally a ship of that size would make do with a replicant engineer and a maintenance crew member. But the Union heavily sanctioned the creation and use of replicants. The Union held the monopoly on replicants. They used them strictly for their own ends. So only ships who in some way either operated for the Union, or were owned by the Union, were allowed replicant crews.

The crew mocked his appearance, his gravelly voice, his slurred speech. He was the odd one out, the man with a robotic arm and a broken face, the dirty one, the Beast, the Monster. In a way he might as well have been a replicant himself for the disregard they showed him.

He ignored them. Their comments didn't bother him. Abe had faced death and beat it enough times to not let a few spiteful remarks get under his skin. He kept his calm. When he reacted, people died. It was that simple. He only needed to maintain a low profile for at least a few more months otherwise he would have killed them all already.

He'd thought to himself, I bet they think they're enduring me. But I'm allowing them to keep on living. I'm enduring them.

They treated him as though he were scum, and he supposed that to them he was. Those clean men and women in their clean white ship, transferring mineral shipments back and forth from the Alpha-Nimoy and Zara-X systems. It was easy work for them and it was easy work for him. Compared to what he normally did it was a holiday, a good rest.

Before taking the job, he had been contacted by a crime boss on the planet Farian, a man known simply as Wang. He offered Abe a lot of money to find his daughter. She'd been kidnapped a few days before by a rival gang. They were trying to move in on Wang's territory, competing to sell narcotic star salts like 4Fave and 3Bz. Abe did a bit of digging, bribing people for information, beating a few to a pulp. He discovered that she was being held in a compound hidden in an area of thick forest on the planet's surface, and that she was guarded by at least twenty men.

Abe piloted a borrowed shuttle to the edge of the forest. He proceeded on foot to the compound. As it turned out, he was a little over-zealous in his plan to blast a hole in the side of the compound with an A10 missile launcher. Not only did it blow half the building away, it killed the girl.

He fled the scene knowing that now he would have both gangs after him. After hiding out for a few days in the busy capital city of Farian, he met a man due to start work as an engineer on-board a ship called the Royale.

He told Abe that he hadn't met his new employer yet and that a friend had set him up with the gig. He bought the guy a few drinks then suggested they switch bars. Abe shuffled him into an alley, killed him and then threw him in a dumpster. Abe knew he would be long gone before anyone discovered the body.

The following morning Abe met the Requisitions Officer of the Royale who reluctantly agreed to take him on. If it had *been for anything else, he wouldn't have been employed. But because Abe looked like a scarred-up engineer with years of experience under his belt, he was taken-on no questions asked. And he could talk the talk. He could always talk the talk.*

30.

The same afternoon, a man sent by Wang tracked him down as he was making arrangements for the contents and cargo of his starship. He couldn't keep hold of the lightweight cruiser now he was a man with a price above his head. The best thing was to disappear for a while. He didn't bear Wang any malice for his reaction. Abe knew he would have dealt with it the same way.

For the first time in many years Abe had failed to carry-through with a job. In the process he'd killed a man's young daughter – an immoral act even by his standards. And for the first time in twice as long, he was hiding. He didn't want to kill Wang, a Father mourning a child.

Abe had murdered, raped, robbed and pillaged. He had double-crossed and back-stabbed and tortured people in the past. But he never willingly killed a child. He was a monster by anyone's standards, but that was one line he never crossed.

Abe made a trip to the hangar where he stored his private starship. After rigging the ship with explosives, he connected a timer which he set to blow once he was safely on board the Royale. With a little luck the explosion would buy him some time before people started asking questions. Starships were like taxis to him. He'd find another soon enough.

Abe was still on his hands and knees under the ship when he heard footsteps crunching on the sandy floor of the hangar. He emerged to find a Klebin male, dressed in light body armour, pointing a long-barrel laser rifle at him.

"Haaands aaaap," he said.

Abe grunted in acknowledgement and put his hands behind his head. "Wang sent yuh?" Abe asked him simply.

The Klebin bared all three rows of his sharp, yellow teeth in a hideous grin. His ghostly white skin wrinkled in a frame around jet black eyes.

"There's a pretty rewaaard for yaaaaa Laroche. Waaaaaang is paying gooood money, and he don't mind yaaaaa being in a body bag either," he said.

Abe shrugged. "Wang's got more savvy than to have me dragged-in alive, mate. That's why he's sent a half-brained dickhead like you to bring me in dead," he said, starting to laugh.

"What aaare ya laughing at?"

"Well, you think you can kill me..." Abe said.

His assassin frowned. "Whadaya mean? Ya think I can't kill yaaa?" he said, agitated, getting a bit closer to Abe and jabbing the rifle in his direction. "Look at ya, Laroche. I have ya at gunpoint. In a second ya head's gonna resemble a-"

That moment of anger, that split second of clouded judgment was all Abe needed. He stepped forward and reached for the barrel of the rifle before the Klebin knew what was happening, twisting to the side as he fired off a few shots reflexively that reverberated in the confined hangar like small atomic explosions. Abe yanked the rifle free of his hands, spun it about and smashed the side of the Klebin's head.

A few pointy teeth flew from his face as the rifle connected with brute force and a soft oomph sound.

"Wahhh!" the Klebin yelled as he stumbled to the left, reaching for his holster and the extra pistol he carried there.

Abe flipped the rifle up and grabbed it by the butt. He slipped his finger over the trigger and blew the Klebin away. The alien hit the other side of the hangar with the full force of the blast. His body slumped against the hangar wall with blue blood bubbling from the giant hole in his midsection. He made a rattling sound from the base of his throat, his hands momentarily grasping for his throat, and then he was still.

Abe tossed the Kelbin's weapon into the open hatch of the ship then collected the alien's body. He bundled him inside the finished setting the timer for the explosives. The body in the wreckage would buy him a few extra hours, maybe an entire day. As Abe emerged from the hangar, he realised he was covered in blue blood. Not the first time, wouldn't be the last.

31.

If the crew knew how he had arrived on board, and of the reputation he had amongst other degenerates and villains such as himself, they wouldn't have taunted him the way they did.

Several days ago they convinced one of the women, a blonde called Lorna, to sleep with Abe so they could secretly film it for their own amusement.

She had come into the engineering room and struck up a friendly conversation. Gradually she moved closer and closer to him, running her hand across his wide, muscled back, feeling the scars that swirled like gnarled bark beneath his oily clothing. She slowly un-buttoned his shirt, kissed his chest, kissed his neck, sucked his bottom lip.

He picked her up, easily, like carrying a child she was so light, and carried her small frame from engineering to his bunk opposite. His room was not as luxurious as those the crew slept in, but he had slept in worse. He had a bunk and a wash basin. He needed little else. He'd lowered her gently on to his mattress and made short work of removing her thin trousers and her uniform top.

She was younger than him, with small breasts that grew erect once he played with them. Little did he know that the rest of the crew had planted a small recording device there in his quarters and had watched the whole thing, as he kissed and slobbered over Lorna. He took her twice; first roughly and savagely with her squealing beneath him, and then slowly, holding her in his arms and kissing her gently as he drove himself powerfully in and out of her.

Intimate contact with a woman was a seldom act for him. Usually he just paid a prostitute when he caught the urge. Every few months he got that aching in his groin, and the impromptu erections that made him have to pay for relief. The women were of differing quality, at both ends of the scale. Women who weren't in the business to charge him to stay in their bed for the night seldom looked his way. He paid to fuck, but the fact was that you couldn't pay anyone to be intimate with you.

He understood how his appearance repulsed most women. He'd been stitched up and put back together so many times, he was completely unrecognizable as the same idealistic and handsome young man who had joined the Terran army all those years before. He'd been fresh-faced, zealous... and very, very naïve back then. That was before Massa E Kym and other battlefields, when the spirit and heart of that young man were blasted to smithereens by the harsh realities of interstellar war.

For Abe the black gulf of years between the man he had been then, to the man he was now, seemed to span centuries. Millennia. Only the stars themselves remained the same.

All of the women aboard the Royale were good looking, petite, all the product of fine breeding and good upbringing. He was of different stock, he knew that. But it hadn't stopped him looking at them as they had passed him, regarding the slight curve of their hips, the gentle motion of their bottoms as they walked about the ship. He noticed Lorna, too, with her golden hair and her soft features.

For people who acted like they were of a higher breed than the humans from the outer colonies, the rest of the crew had certainly gone lower than he'd have thought them capable of when they convinced Lorna to sleep with him for their amusement.

After he finished, Abe had rose from the bed and handed her a towel.

"Use that if yuh like," he said.

She smiled at him politely, but had a strange look on her face. She seemed so eager to sleep with him, and had certainly been game when he brought her to his

222

quarters. He knew when a woman was excited, and he knew that she was genuinely excited, and ready, to sleep with him when he'd stripped her off. Now she looked as though she were ashamed of herself. As he stood dressing himself and watching her clean herself up, it struck Abe that Lorna had the same look that so many of the prostitutes he slept with had when he finished... sexually satisfied, but left feeling dirty.

He had grown a thick skin against the repulsion he saw on their faces after sleeping with him and in the same manner he dismissed Lorna's expression as just another example of that repulsion. It was a bit like eating a seafood dinner and then remembering that you didn't like fish.

As she stood to dress herself, Lorna said "I've got to get to the Command Centre."

"Yuh," he said.

A few hours later he went to the mess to fix himself something to eat, and he found most of the crew in there laughing and joking. They quieted when he walked in, and when he looked at the vid screen he saw why. There he was, driving himself in and out of Lorna on his bunk, grunting like an animal. He looked from the vid screen and then at the crew as they started to laugh again.

"Really fucking funny," Abe said, the vein in the side of his neck pulsating.

They laughed even more. One of the male crewmembers, Cooper, rewound the footage back to when Abe had been pulling his clothes off, a big grin on his face. He laughed as the footage played, and he sounded like a jackal. Abe saw red and lunged for Cooper, grabbing him by the neck with his metal arm and lifting him up till his feet dangled off of the floor. Cooper grabbed for the place around his neck where Abe's artificial hand was closing, gripping hard.

"Funny now?" Abe asked through gritted teeth.

Lorna stepped out from amongst the crew, and Abe looked at her, knowing that the planting of the recording device in his quarters had not been orchestrated by the crew alone.

"Stop!" she shouted at him.

Cooper was turning purple. Abe released his grip and Cooper dropped to the floor. The other crew rushed to Cooper's aid, their demeanour completely changed from when Abe walked in only moments before. The humour had left the room. On the vid display, Abe was on top of Lorna, his breathing heavy.

He looked across at Lorna. For a split second he thought he saw... what? Guilt?

Any other time, *Abe thought*, I would have snapped his neck.

He would have smashed the vid screen too if he knew he wouldn't end up spending hours replacing it after. Without saying a word Abe left the mess room and headed for his quarters. He located the recording device and crushed it in his mechanical hand, reducing the small box to a crumpled fistful of black scrap. Then he returned to the engine room, expecting a visit from Captain Anderson for what he'd done to Cooper, but not receiving one.

Sitting on his bunk that night, replaying the love making, the embarrassment of them all laughing about it and the incident with Cooper, he contemplated invading the crew's quarters and doing some damage to Cooper to make an example of him. Perhaps maul him. Grab his face and squeeze his head until his eyeballs started to pop from the sockets. Eventually he convinced himself to lie down and let it go.

He let it go, sure. But he hadn't forgotten it.

32.

Abe sat in the engine room, in the dark, listening to the sounds of shouting and screaming on the upper decks. This went on for several minutes then nothing. The ship was more or less silent save for the continual grinding of the reactor gears and the gurgling of the coolant pipes in the engine room.

The comm panel on the wall beeped. Abe got up and walked over to it. He had a direct call from the officer's mess.

Abe hit the **RECEIVE** button.

It was Captain Anderson. The senior officer of the ship. Abe hadn't seen much of him since coming aboard. Whilst the ship was in transit the Captain preferred to remain in his quarters doing God-knows-what. Abe had heard talk of Anderson building model ships. Grown men playing with toys was an alien concept to Abe. He had wondered whether Anderson knew what the crew got up to whilst he hid himself away in luxury.

"Frank? You there?" the Captain's voice sounded frayed, stressed. "Engineer?" Whatever happened must have surprised Anderson, too, because he sounded pushed.

Abe smiled.

"Yuh. Here."

"Where have you been? The ship's been overrun. The enemy has taken over the command centre."

By the enemy he meant the Draxx, of course.

"I'm in engineering," Abe said simply.

"Thank God. We're locked in the mess at the moment. They locked us all in here after they breached the airlock. I don't think they had the foresight to disable the internal comm stations. At least they didn't execute us…" Anderson said.

Abe grunted.

"You need to come and get us out of here, Frank, on the double."

Abe nodded but didn't say anything.

"Frank?"

"Yuh. Still here."

Anderson sighed.

"Frank we need to get to the lifeboat. It has enough room and supplies for all of us, and it might be our only chance of escaping this ship. Once they've got what they want, they'll blow this ship up with us in it. That's how they operate. You know that?"

"Yuh," Abe said. He knew it.

Trouble is, *he thought,* do you have any idea how I fucking operate?

Abe heard frightened voices in the background.

Those fuckers, *he thought to himself.* Quivering in their boots like children. If only I had footage of that!

In the pitch black, thinking of them frightened half to death, he grinned as if he were darkness incarnate.

"Come and get us Frank," Anderson said. "You're our only hope."

"Yuh," Abe replied and closed the comm channel.

33.

Abe sparked a welding torch so he could see in the pitch black, and walked back to the reactor. He cut through several of the coolant control pipes and then turned the torch on the pressure control panel. The reactor whined as its temperature rose from lack of coolant.

If the Draxx came into the engine room and discovered his sabotage they wouldn't have the time to fix the pipes, nor would they be able to shut down the reactor. In case they tried to disable it manually, he also welded the emergency levers so they couldn't be turned. He had locked the ship into a cycle of overload and it was so simple. The ship would explode once the reactor reached critical temperature.

It wouldn't take long.

He listened for noise outside the engine room entrance before venturing outside and climbing the ladder to the main corridor. There were no Draxx about, none patrolling.

They're confident they have everyone locked up, *he thought.*

Red emergency lighting flashed in his eyes and the klaxons that the Draxx hadn't silenced emitted a low wail.

He padded along the corridor, making his way to the aft of the ship. As he passed the crew's quarters, he heard a thump come from one of them. The door was locked. He forced it open with his robotic arm. He found Lorna on the floor, hugging her knees.

She wailed as he walked in and pulled her to her feet.

"Come!" he growled at her.

She stopped screaming.

"Come!" he said again, dragging her into the corridor.

"Where are the others?" she asked him.

"Locked up in the officer's mess."

"Oh God..." She said, clinging to him as they walked.

They came to the intersection that would take them to the left, to the mess room, the gym, and the medical bays, and to the right which led to the hangar deck. He paused at the corner. Lorna attempted to press ahead but he shoved her back. When she looked up he held one finger to his lips. Peering around the corner he saw a Draxx foot soldier pulling apart a wall panel, throwing wires and circuitry everywhere.

The Draxx was at least eight feet tall, with a long snout filled with small but sharp teeth. Its thick tail swished from side to side, as it tore at the wall panel with its clawed hands. It had brown armour about its chest, and a belt with daggers and a pistol attached to it. Abe left Lorna cowering around the corner and crept towards the reptile. As he closed in, the Draxx turned towards him.

Abe leapt on it, wrapping his mechanical arm about its neck. With his other arm he reached for the pistol on the reptile's belt. The Draxx bucked and tried to toss him off, turning in circles and screaming with a hair-raising roar. The Draxx struggled to sink its claws into Abe. If it did, it would tear him to bits. He pulled the pistol free of the belt and jabbed it into the Draxx's side.

He fired.

An eruption of clear fluid and yellow flesh flew from the creature's torso, splatting up the wall. He fired again and again until it dropped to the floor. Abe rose to his feet and fired once more at the Draxx's twitching body.

Abe returned to where Lorna sat shivering and staring wide-eyed at the wall. He grabbed her by the arm. He checked the path to the hangar deck, then turned right, dragging Lorna along with him.

"That... that... thing..." Lorna muttered.

"A Draxx," Abe said, pulling her with him. *"Don't worry about it. It's dead now."*

Lorna gaped at the corpse as he pulled her past it. In her slightly dazed state she realised where he was leading her.

"Where are we going?" Lorna asked him.

"To the lifeboat. We're getting off this ship," he said.

He made her move quickly down the ladder that led to the hangar. There was another way of getting to the lifeboat, but it meant using the main entrance and he didn't want to expose himself like that if there were Draxx in the hangar bay. He climbed down after her. The two of them reached the floor of the hangar behind several large cargo containers. He peeked around one of them and found the hangar empty. He didn't know what the Draxx were after, but they weren't looking for it this end of the ship. It wasn't cargo they sought.

The lifeboat sat in the middle of the hangar. It was a large saucer shape with a pointed front and a cluster of small engines at the back.

"Up!" he said to Lorna. He yanked her arm and dragged her towards the lifeboat. He accessed the controls to the entrance and stood back as it slid open. He shoved Lorna inside first and then climbed in himself.

Abe watched the entrance hatch close automatically behind them and then he mounted the flight controls.

Inside the ship were places for up to twelve people. Lorna sat in one of the seats and buckled herself in. As Abe started the engines, she spoke.

"I thought you were saving the others, not leaving them there."

He said nothing.

Abe flipped a few switches. The bay doors opened. A rush of air flew past the front viewport, sucked into the vacuum of space. Abe brought the engines online and *eased the lifeboat forward. The tiny vessel cleared the bay doors in seconds.*

"Why have you left them behind?" she asked him.

He ignored her. They left the Royale behind.

"We have to go back for them!" she shouted at him.

When they'd come a safe distance from the Royale, he cut the engines and spun them about so they faced the ship and the large spherical Draxx ship hanging from it like a tumor. Seconds later there was a bright white flash and both ships blew apart. The lifeboat was rocked by the resultant shockwave, the overhead lights flickering.

"You're a monster..." Lorna said, although he suspected she was not as sad about her companions' deaths as she made out.

Abe shrugged.

He'd been called a monster before.

"Look, love, there was no way we could rescue the others. The ship was overrun. And I wasn't risking my skin even trying."

Lorna nodded.

"So you would have left me as well," she said.

Abe grinned at her. "Don't matter, does it? Found yuh so no need to grumble," he said.

There was a moment of silence between them.

"Now what?" she asked him, slumping back in her chair.

"A planet called Ractor Prime in the Alpha-Nimoy system, about three weeks journey from here. We might just have enough rations and fuel to get us there... if we're lucky," he said.

Lorna rolled her eyes. "Three weeks!"

Just a spoiled brat like the rest of them, *he thought.* I knew her concern for the others was just an act.

"I can't believe I'm trapped in this tin can with you for three whole fucking weeks!" she said, releasing herself from the safety harness and standing up.

Abe remembered Lorna standing with the others in the officer's mess as the footage played of him grunting on top of her. She had stood there, laughing with them. Laughing at him. Her mutual affection towards him as he had nailed her had seemed so genuine.

He stood up. Lorna watched, startled, as Abe started to unbuckle his trousers. She saw the Beast in all its glory.

Abe had a considerable appetite, and food would not abate it, as Lorna came to realise.

34.

"I'm not proud of what happened," Abe said. He searched Sara's face for a reaction. An indicator of how she was taking it.

"Do you believe me, that I'm capable of that remorse?" Abe asked.

Sara nodded, slowly. "It's just a lot to take in. I knew you had a murky past, you know. Anyone could guess it from your tattoos and scars. But..."

Abe held out his hand to her. She took it, hesitantly.

"I've been a monster. They call me The Tattooed Man. A nameless terror. But that's in the past. I'm putting it all behind me," he said.

"Yes, and what about the people on that ship? *The Royale*? What about them?" Sara asked.

Abe couldn't answer.

* * *

He walked her outside to the skimmer. The night sky was clear and filled with stars. He helped her up. "Yuh must be pretty disgusted with me right now," he said.

Sara's face was dark and unreadable. "I'm not disgusted. I don't know what to feel. It's a lot. Sometimes you see a big black hole in the ground. You wonder how far down it goes, and when you find out, you wish you'd never wondered such a thing. Just let it be what it is. A big black hole. I think you're sort of like that, Abe. One of life's mysteries it might be better not knowing about," she said.

"Then maybe you have to accept me as that," Abe said.

"Maybe... Doesn't stop you *being* it though, does it?" she said.

Abe wasn't sure what to say to that. He didn't expect anybody to accept what he'd done in the past. In fact he thought Sara would run for the hills. But she didn't. She just had a lot to digest right now. If she did accept it, he knew that one day he would feel free to bare his soul to her, confess each and every sin. He hoped that would be the case. He needed someone to listen to him. All his life he'd never felt that need to unload the burden of his past, but now he did.

He had a chance at renewal, at redemption, and he was committed to take it.

It wasn't going to be easy.

"Abe."

He snapped to. Sara looked to the sky. Instantly he spotted a thin white trail that flew starward as it left the planet behind.

"Is that a ship?" she asked, their conversation forgotten.

"I don't know. Could be a probe," he said. "Get back to camp, love. Tell them it looks like we've been found."

She looked frightened. "What does that mean?"

Abe took a deep breath. "It means we need to get out of here as soon as possible," he said. He watched her leave and then looked up at the stars overhead, watching.

He stood there a long time.

35.

The Union Battleship 'Attila' T.U.6641

"Slow to Galactic Standard," Admiral Royce ordered. The Attila's Captain repeated the order to the lower ranks.

The Rishi Drift lay before them, a gaseous area of space that flashed with eruptions of energy. Dangerous and volatile.

"Full alert, Captain. I want all available power routed to the energy shields," Royce ordered.

"Yes Admiral."

Again, Royce listened with satisfaction as his wishes were carried down the chain of command. He didn't often exert his control over the running of the ship. He allowed Captain Perez to do what he had to.

But he was anxious to get through the Rishi Drift in one piece and slipped into the Commanding Officer habits of the past.

The Tattooed Man was down on that planet. They just had to get through the Drift first. Then he would have the galaxy's most wanted man within his grasp. The probe had confirmed the presence of a humanoid settlement on the surface. He was sure that the Tattooed Man was down there. He was most likely with them. Or he had come across a settlement and murdered them all, keeping the resources for himself. Royce didn't put anything past such a monster.

He would not get away this time. He'd face the penalty for his crimes.

"Captain, be sure to tell the engineer to push the generators to one hundred and twenty-five percent output. Maximum efficiency. And have all fighters stand by at the ready."

"Aye aye, Admiral," Perez said.

Royce surveyed the space in front of them. They neared the edges of the Drift and he knew it would be a rough journey making it through. But worth it.

I'm coming for you, he thought.

36.

It was still dark out when they arrived at the ship. Half an hour later Paul called a meeting.

"Right, let's see how this thing's going to pan out," Paul said. They stood around a table in the mess room aboard the *Neberkenezer*. It was cramped in there, but the key players of the group just about squeezed in. He had a crude map of the surrounding space laid out on the table-top held down on each corner by nuts and bolts.

"We are surrounded by the Drift. There's no avoiding it. I'd like to, trust me," he said.

He tapped the top right corner of the map he'd made. "Sensors indicate a presence here. Laurie detected it an hour or so ago."

Laurie spoke up. "I picked up on an energy signature in that area. Could be anything. But seeing as Abe is certain he saw a probe leaving the surface last night, we can be sure it's something to do with the Union."

"A small ship?" Sara asked.

Laurie shrugged. "I can't tell. Not at this distance. I'd be inclined to agree with Abe. It's probably a probe of some type. The Drift kicks out quite a bit of radiation, swamping the sensors. It's a bit like peering through fog."

"If they're here because of me," Abe said, "Then you can expect them to come at us full measures. However..."

"Yes?" Paul said.

"They *will* want me alive. I'm a wanted man, they're going to want to try and get me alive first. And that might give us an advantage," he said.

"You mean they won't blow us out the sky straight away, they'll stop to ask questions first," Paul said.

Abe nodded. "Yuh."

The others looked. Abe now felt guilty he had brought all of this to their doorstep, that he was forcing their departure from the planet they'd called home for so long. But it couldn't be helped, and they needed to get a move on as much as he did.

Besides, he considered his own destiny to be intertwined with theirs now.

"Well that gives us something. I'm hoping that we can move quickly enough to run before we get shot at," Paul said.

"We're cycling the main generator now. We should be at full power within the hour," Court said.

"And you're certain the Jump Drive is going to work?" Paul asked.

"With the modifications Abe's helped us with, I can't see why not," Laurie said.

Paul laughed. "We're going to have to hit the ground running, for sure."

"Pretty much," Laurie said.

"When we escape the atmosphere, we need to head in the opposite direction of whatever presence we have on our sensors. And we need to run with everything we've got. Laurie's gonna be monitoring the ship overall, watching for anything that decides to die on us. Court will be working with the Jump Drive," Abe said. "But it'll all be for nothing if we can't get beyond the Drift to use it."

"Sara will be on hand in a medical capacity, of course. Stape and Myself will run things from the bridge," Paul said. "What will you be doing?"

Abe wagged a finger playfully. "A little surprise. Something they won't expect. But I need a bit more time to get it ready for our departure... time we don't have. It's gonna be cutting it close."

Paul pulled in a deep breath, stood to full height. "Then my friends, let's get a move on. Laurie, you're saying we can have full power within the hour. So let's say an hour from now we need to get up in the air. Agreed?"

They all murmured their agreement.

"Take what you can with you. Make sure that everyone who isn't doing something has a seat somewhere and is strapped into it. If they're not needed for something, don't let them get in the way," Paul said.

"A good point," Abe said.

Paul looked to Sara. "For some of us, this is going to be time to say our farewells."

She looked down at the ground. Court put an arm about her. Somewhere in the bowel of the ship there came a *chime chime chime* sound, as if someone were literally ringing the bells of change.

"Okay. Let's not waste any more time. We've got too much to do, and not enough time to do it. Let's see if we can get out of here before the sun comes up. Good luck everyone."

37.

"Quickly! Quickly!"

Paul ushered in the last of the refugees, stepped back inside the ship and grabbed the back of the door. He paused for a moment to look across the landscape at the place they had called home for nearly twenty years. A part of him felt gutted for having to leave it, as crazy as that seemed.

He slammed the door shut, then the inner door. A control panel gave him quick access to the pressure seals.

Now they were all locked in.

The rumble of the engines shook the entire ship, sending tremors down its length as he walked to the nearest comm unit and spoke into it.

"This is Paul. We are clear for launch. Repeat. Clear for launch."

He wanted more time, not only to bid farewell to their home but to prepare the rest of the group for what would come next. The galaxy was a big place, and they would have to find their place within it. Somehow.

He doubted they would get away with settling down somewhere and living a quiet existence. The Union knew that Abe was with them, and they would soon know who *he* was with. Then the Union would hunt them. And its resources were endless.

He passed rooms of people huddled around each other. The engines built to full strength. A jolt that shook the entire ship from aft to stern sent him reeling against a bulkhead. He gripped the cool metal, pulled himself straight and continued forward to the bridge.

Stape was absorbed in getting the *Neberkenezer* in the air. His fingers flew expertly across the controls. Abe was on the floor, bundles of wires pooled around his hands from one of the consoles. He clipped two ends together.

"There yuh go fella. Try that," he called over to Stape.

Stape pushed forward on a lever and the *Neberkenezer* moved through the sky.

"Yes! We did it!" Stape yelled.

Abe stood up, his hand falling heavily on Stape's shoulder. "Keep yuh cool lad. Fly 'er straight."

Although there was no chair for the captain, there was a safety bar across the ceiling. Paul grabbed ahold of it as the *Neberkenezer* tilted back and rocketed through the atmosphere.

"I'm going back," Abe said. He turned to Paul as he left the bridge. "Don't let him take her up too fast mate. Ease her in. Give me a few minutes before we push her hard. I'll call forward."

"Okay Abe," Paul said.

When the bulkhead door slammed shut behind him, Paul turned to Stape and told him to take her steady.

* * *

Abe ran down to the engineering section. "We all right girls?"

Court had her hands full. The Jump Drive unit flickered with energy that continued to build. The light from the unit filled all of engineering. It threatened to make Court a mere silhouette. "Jump Drive is nearly there, Abe," she said.

"Good girl. Keep your eye on it. Laurie?" Abe asked.

Laurie looked up from where she was stationed, monitoring the readouts of the ships various functions. "All good here. He's breaking her in slowly. So far so good," she said.

Abe nodded. He moved to a section of wiring and circuitry that he had left open and exposed. Amidst all of the mess he had been tying in the device that he and Paul retrieved from the alien ship. There were still connections to be made before it would operate correctly. *I so fucking hope this thing works,* he thought to himself. *Or we're dead in the water.*

Before he got to the floor to work on it, he stamped the comm panel with his palm and opened a line. "Bridge, Abe."

"Go ahead," Paul said.

"You can take her up now boss. Everything looks good from here," Abe reported.

"Okay Abe. Taking her up."

Abe looked from Court to Laurie. A cheeky devils smirk danced across his lips. "No turning back now girls," he said.

This time Laurie didn't look up from her controls. "Time to start clenching arse cheeks then," she said.

* * *

"Take her up Stape," Paul said.

Stape pushed the old ship to full speed. She tore through the atmosphere and the ground rushed away. They did not have the liberty of ascending slowly and leisurely. The whole idea was to get into space as quickly as possible, get through the Drift, then fire up the Jump Drive. Get out of dodge.

Paul gripped the bar too tightly as they rocketed starward. The front end of the ship shuddered from the cut of aged metal through freezing cold atmosphere. He grimaced as they tilted even further back, and when he thought Stape couldn't push the old girl any more, he did. She was like lightning and before he knew it, the blue was fading to black and they were in space.

Now we see, Paul thought.

38.

The Union Battleship 'Attila' T.U.6641

"Captain! One ship entering the Drift," Ensign Rogers called from the front of the bridge.

"Configuration?" Admiral Perez asked.

"It appears to be Draxx, with some modifications from other craft. I'm getting a mixed reading sir, but it's mostly Draxx."

Perez turned to Admiral Royce.

"Admiral, we should pursue them now before we risk losing them in the Drift," Perez said.

"Launch a squadron, Captain. But tell them I want that ship in one piece," Royce ordered. "And Captain... go with them. Take my personal fighter."

Perez snapped to attention, giving Royce a full salute in compliance.

"I am honored, sir!"

Royce clasped his hands behind his back and regarded Perez with mock respect.

"I am trusting you to oversee the pursuit personally, Captain. Don't fail me," he warned him.

Perez nodded in the affirmative, turned on his heels and left with speed.

Royce turned back to the many read-outs and watched the steady blip of the enemy craft making its way across one of the big screens.

A minute or so later, Ensign Rogers reported that the Admiral's fighter had left the hangar bay. He nodded in acknowledgement.

39.

"Yuh. That's it." Abe said, to himself. "That's it yuh fucker!"

He slammed in the last power cable, watched the device hum to life. It glowed a strange, alien orange from one end. It was working. Court and Laurie were looking over in his direction.

The comm unit crackled to life.

"Abe. We're getting strange readings up here. Is everything okay down there?"

He stood up, walked over to the unit.

"Yuh. Fine. I just got my little surprise juiced up is all," he said, pleased with himself.

"Our short range sensors have been knocked out," Paul said.

"Yuh. I thought they might. Long range is still working though, right?"

After a second Paul confirmed they were.

"That's fine then. It's a small price to pay. Tell Stape he's gotta drive with his eyes open," Abe said.

"What is *that device Abe?"*

"No time to explain right now, but it's a cloaking device," Abe said.

"You mean we're invisible?" Laurie asked, gob-smacked.

Abe crossed his arms in front of his chest, proud of himself, without even realising he was doing it.

"Cool," Court said.

"Will it hold?" Paul asked.

Abe shrugged, as if Paul could see him.

"Don't know mate. It might. It might not. But it'll throw 'em if they're already onto us. Might buy us some time."

* * *

"They're gone sir!" Rogers said, staring incredulously at his readouts.

Confusion clouded Royce's brow. "What do you *mean* they're gone?"

"One minute they were there, sir, and the next... gone. I can't understand it."

Royce's lips set in a thin white line. "Find them."

* * *

Captain Perez held tight formation with the rest of the fighter squadron. He pressed two fingers against the side of his helmet as he spoke into it.

"We'll find them Admiral," he said.

He placed both hands on his flight controls, pushed the Admiral's fighter to full speed.

"Stay in formation. Full acceleration. Visual recon," he ordered.

They signalled in one by one confirming his orders.

"Hold your fire until I give the word," he said.

* * *

"We're getting into the thick of the Drift. The long range readings show massive energy discharges in there," Stape said.

"Well we don't have a choice," Paul said.

"And there's something else," Stape said as he looked down at his readouts. "I'm seeing a grouping of ships headed our way."

Paul drew in a deep breath. "Then let's not hang around, Stape. Push her hard as you can."

40.

"See those storms?" Stape said He nodded at what was racing up ahead of them. Paul stood behind him.

"Yes. Just like before," Paul said, grimly.

The vast nebulous structure of the Drift flashed with shotgun blasts of energy discharge that filled the bridge with ghostly white light.

"If any of that hits us..." Stape said nervously.

"I know," Paul interjected. He didn't need to hear it.

Stape drew in a deep breath, settled in his seat. His hands flew over the controls as he steered the ship in and around pockets of destructive nebula and rocky debris.

"Easy goes," Paul said, his hands gripping the back of the pilot's chair until his knuckles turned white with pressure.

The *Neberkenezer* groaned in the same way an athlete groans when he goes for a run after too long away from the track. The old ship had been thrown back into active duty, and she seemed to ache as she was put through her paces. A large chunk of planetoid pirouetted through space immediately in front of them, and Stape struggled to bring the *Neberkenezer*'s nose down quickly enough to avoid it. They barely skimmed past it. The proximity alarms wailed.

"Bridge, Engineering. Everything all right up there?" it was Laurie over the comm.

Paul walked to the panel, jabbed his finger against the button. "Yeah fine. Don't worry about us."

A massive bolt of energy erupted in front of the ship. It cut across its path as two areas of cloud discharged simultaneously.

Paul lifted a hand to shield his eyes. Luckily the bolt dispersed seconds before they ploughed through it. The area of charged particles it left in its wake caused the hull to sizzle.

"God," Paul said. He looked up, almost expected the inner skin of the hull to drip molten and red hot from the ceiling.

"I hope that's as close as it gets," Stape said.

* * *

Captain Perez scanned the vast Drift with his eyes as he cut swiftly around whatever lay in his path. He was a skilled pilot, or he had been back in the day. It pleased him that none of that changed over the years. It felt like slipping into a pair of old shoes.

"Open up," he said into his comm unit. "Spread out."

He watched the other ships move apart and fan out across his vector to widen the net. You first opened the net and spread it wide to entrap your quarry then you tightened it, like a hangman's noose.

"Where are you?" he said.

* * *

"So what are we going to do when we get out of here?" Stape asked, his face set in concentration.

"Abe's planted the seeds of something, since he's been with us," Paul said.

"Oh yeah?"

"Yes," Paul said. "A notion. Something that could change it for all of us."

Stape glanced over his shoulder quickly. "D'you mean..."

Paul slapped him on the shoulder. "Exactly that. We've millions of brothers and sisters out there, all slaves to the Union.

I think it's about time they were given their freedom. I think-"

He was thrown sidewards. A huge arc of energy tore past the *Neberkenezer*, knocked it starboard. Paul grabbed the edge of a console to steady himself. Stape struggled with the controls and fought the ship to keep her level.

"Did it hit?"

Stape shook his head. "Grazed us. It was close. Too close."

Paul peered ahead, at a large cluster of dark clouds that gurgled with bitter white light. Before he could say *that looks dangerous*, a blast of energy erupted from them and headed straight for the *Neberkenezer*.

"Stape-!" he managed to yell before he lost his grip. He slammed against the far wall. His head smacked against metal. Stars whirled in front of his eyes. He nearly blacked out but he fought it off.

The ship spun then listed to one side. The lights flickered on and off as the power fluctuated. Unconsciousness crept in at the edges, and Paul pushed it back. *Gotta get up,* he thought. *Can't shut my eyes.*

He reached up, grabbed ahold of something, got to his feet. His legs were like jelly and his head spun almost as much as the ship, but he could stand.

* * *

The ship came out of nowhere. Perez couldn't believe his luck.

"All fighters, converge on target! Pincer formation!"

He grinned from ear to ear.

The ship that had left the ice planet shimmered from some kind of shielding. He suspected stealth technology. There was no other way they could have snuck past without him spotting them. He glanced down at his sensor display and could see the ship quite clearly. It hadn't been there before.

He moved to within a few lengths of it before he brought the Admiral's ship to a stop. The other fighters encircled it, at a distance. Tightened the noose.

The enemy ship... the one that had the Tattooed Man aboard had stopped spinning but still listed like an injured soldier. A section of the hull along the top side of the ship, where the energy bolt had connected was blackened and charred. Something spewed from it in a fine spray of yellow sparks like welding slag. From so close, Perez could see the lights within the ship wax and wane.

"Hold positions," he said into his comm unit. "And hold your fire unless I order that you do different."

He switched to another channel, one that he knew the enemy ship would pick up.

"Enemy vessel. You are under arrest. Respond, over."

41.

Abe moved swiftly in the darkness to help Laurie and Court patch the *Neberkenezer* back together. Or at least get her on the move again. The hit had knocked out the main power contactors for a start. The bridge had minimal helm control. They were sitting ducks.

"Abe! They're contacting us," Paul said on the comm

Abe grunted next to Court as they re-wired two engineering consoles and quickly connected them together for a tenuous fix of the helm problem. Stape could at least bring the ship back under control.

"What do we do?" Paul asked.

"Fuck sake," Abe muttered under his breath. He walked to the comm unit and slammed his fist against it. "Just keep 'em guessing. Don't answer 'em," he snapped.

Paul didn't answer.

He turned back to Court. "Get that conductor over there, Court. Tie it in."

She did as he instructed. Across the rest of the ship the lighting and life support came on and off, but in engineering they had only an emergency lantern to illuminate their efforts.

"Laurie, how's that doing?"

She was on the upper level. She hastily replaced a board that had burst into flame when they got hit.

"Won't be long," she said, buried in her work.

Good. Don't think we've got long either, Abe thought.

* * *

Perez could feel his patience begin to slip. "Enemy vessel. Respond."

Nothing. No answer from them. But he could have sworn he saw movement from within, when the lights were on. He wondered what they were doing in there. Beyond, deep within the Drift a series of lightning bursts went off, flashing in tandem. He didn't see the one that hit them, but he knew that was why they had lost their shielding.

He sighed. Spoke into the comm again. "Enemy vessel. *Respond*."

* * *

Everything lit up like a christmas tree, all at once. Stape lifted his hands away from the helm console as though it were hot. "Whoa!"

Paul grinned, clapped his hands together.

"Right! Back in business!"

He spoke to Abe in engineering. "Abe! Good job!"

"Don't thank me, mate. Thank the girls."

"Abe-" he started but Abe broke through.

"Hold that thought. I've gotta come up."

Paul didn't say anything. He opened the bulkhead door and listened to Abe's footfall as he ran to the bridge. For a big man he was light on his feet.

"That was quick," Paul said.

Abe strode onto the bridge, walked straight to the tactical station and assessed their situation. They had them pinned in on all sides. Well... nearly.

"They don't figure on us flying over their heads," Abe said, almost to himself.

"What's that?" Paul asked.

Abe illustrated with his hands. "We fly up and over them, like this."

Paul nodded. "And head for open space," he said.

"The stealth is fucked though mate. Sorry," Abe said.

Paul opened his mouth to speak, but the comm from the engineering crackled into life again.

"Abe. Paul. We've got a problem. A big one." It was Court.

Abe looked from Paul to Stape then walked to the unit. His throat went dry. "Go on."

* * *

They both stood in engineering and listened to Court deliver the bad news. Laurie was still up on the upper level but she leant over the railing and listened. They were both covered in sweat and grime. The engineering section was hot and sticky, filled with the tang of burnt plastic and wiring.

"...so unless we can get the external feed reconnected, we're pretty much screwed," Court said. She looked from one to the other, hoping for an answer.

Abe hung his head. The power lines that ran the length of the ship - that fed the Jump Drive unit - were severed when the ship was hit. Unlike most systems on board, it couldn't be bypassed from within. There was only one option: go outside and fix it. Abe knew he could do it.

But he knew what that meant.

Nobody said anything for what seemed like an age, until Abe looked up at them all and broke the silence. "I'll do it."

"You can't do that Abe," Laurie said from above him. "There's no guarantee we'd get you back inside the ship before we jumped."

"Yuh I know that," Abe said.

* * *

They held a quick meeting, there in the engineering section. Paul collected Sara so she could be privy to the discussion. He also thought she deserved to be there, to hear what Abe proposed. Over the time Abe had been with them, he had seen the two of them grow close. After the loss of Jax it had pleased Paul to see her opening up to someone.

They had all spent so long alone, in many ways.

But now it seemed that all of that would change again.

"I've supplied Paul with the co-ordinates of a little place I have. It's a deserted base from the Outland Wars, and I've called it home for decades. There you'll find credits, supplies, weapons, and a few contacts in my database that might come in handy for yuh all," Abe said.

Paul watched Sara. How she reacted. But none of it showed, not yet.

"Stape could level the ship, but he's letting her drift to buy us some time. They won't wait forever though, which is why we need to move now. Make a run for it, head for open space. Hopefully by the time you get there I'll have the Drive fixed."

"Won't they try to stop us?" Laurie asked him.

Abe shook his head.

"Not right away. They'll give chase but they won't open fire unless they really have to, and if they do they'll aim for the engines. Yuh know, shoot the legs off the runner sorta thing," he said.

"You know there are two suits aboard, Abe," Paul said.

"This only needs one," Abe said.

Paul stepped forward. "But it will be quicker with two of us, won't it?"

Abe sighed. "Yuh," he said simply.

Paul asked Laurie and Court to leave the room for a moment, to help him prep the suits. He gave Abe and Sara a moment of privacy he knew they needed.

* * *

"You're a brave man," Sara said.

She stepped toward him, took his massive mitts in hers, squeezed them tight.

"I'm doing what I gotta do," he said.

She kissed him on the chin, and he closed his eyes, savoring the feel of her soft lips against his skin. Instantly he thought of Lorna. He couldn't help it. A part of him wished that he could wipe her clean from his memory, from his heart... but that was the same part of him keeping hold of her.

She wrapped her arms around him, snuggled in, sighed.

"You *will* come back," she said.

He swallowed. "Yuh," he lied.

"I'm glad you came into our lives, Abe," she said, looking up into his eyes. "You showed us humanity, even when you thought you had none left."

He didn't know how to react. Should he say something? Cry?

Instead he simply held her, tight. He savoured it. A single moment stretched out until it seemed to last forever... and then the others were back to tell Abe it was time to go.

* * *

Paul explained the whole plan to Stape. "As soon as you see the airlock is engaged, you start flying us out of here. Don't wait around. And don't worry about us, we'll be fine."

Abe was already getting into his suit.

"Good luck," Stape said.

Paul walked briskly to the rear of the ship, to get into his suit as quickly as possible. He found one of the men, Harmer, on the floor holding his head.

He dropped to the floor beside him.

"My God, Harmer, what happened? Where's Abe?" he asked.

Harmer had a small trickle of blood making its way down his forehead from where he'd been hit.

"Hit me before I knew it," Harmer said. "Then he did *that*."

He pointed to the other space suit. The front visor of the helmet had been smashed in, the material on the suit slashed with a knife.

"I failed you," Harmer said over and over as he clutched his head.

Paul walked to the nearest comm unit and hit the SEND button. "Stape, this is Paul. Get us out of here. Fast as you can."

42.

Perez watched as the *Neberkenezer* righted itself and slowly rose upward. Before he had time to open his mouth, the ships engines erupted into life and it rocketed away.

"All ships! Follow, follow, follow!" he yelled.

He threw the levers forward, leading the chase. As he piloted around incoming debris he hurriedly patched himself through to the *Attilla*.

* * *

"Very well Captain. Do what you must," Royce said, closing the channel.

So the Tattooed Man was making a run for it, with Perez and the others in pursuit.

One of the most wanted men in the galaxy... he was never going to come quietly, was he?

"Sir, sensors indicate they are headed for the edge of the Drift. It appears as if they are making for open space," Rogers reported.

Admiral Royce clasped his hands behind his back.

"Take us out of the Drift, on a direct intercept course. I want to wait outside the warren for when the rabbit comes running."

"Aye Aye Sir!" Rogers yelled, relaying the order to the helmsman.

Immediately the great battleship turned on its axis and headed back out the way it came, ready to catch the *Neberkenezer* when it emerged from the Drift.

* * *

"All ships, hold fire until my order. Do not follow my lead," Perez ordered. He levelled his sights on the rear of the *Neberkenezer*, then allowed it to drift to starboard before opening fire. Rapid-fire Neutron Shells shot forth from the main cannon. They skimmed past the hull. He stayed tight as the *Neberkenezer* threw its hips from left to right, following standard evasive procedure. He expected nothing less.

"Bastard," Perez muttered under his breath.

Every time they levelled back out, he sprayed them with fire. He was trying very hard not to hit them. Not yet. But he would do, and his aim was true.

* * *

There were rungs built into the hull, running from one side to the other to accommodate extra-vehicular activity. With the ship throwing him this way and that, Abe had to hold on for dear life as his body lifted away from the hull, his legs dangling. It was a good thing he had a strong grip. And a robotic arm that would never let out. Anyone with lesser strength would have been thrown into space, with no means of getting back. Game over.

Abe held onto the power mountings with his artificial hand whilst he worked on it with his other. It wasn't as bad as he'd feared. But it wasn't easy, riding the back of a giant metal whale.

The enemy fire wasn't helping either. Another round of them flew past him, nearly striking. He grimaced.

Getting pissed now, he thought. *Fuck this.*

Before getting his helmet on, Abe had retrieved several of his own weapons from one of the quarters on the *Neberkenezer*. He had a heavy rifle loaded with Quantum rounds strapped to his side, alongside a mesh pouch filled with thermal grenades.

He got to his feet, balancing on the hull, and unclipped the heavy rifle. He turned to face the big fighter and leveled the rifle at it.

"Yuh bastard!" he yelled. He squeezed down on the trigger and opened fire.

The fighter didn't see it coming. Abe's fire impacted directly against the front of the ship in multiple explosions. He grinned from ear to ear, never happier than when he was unleashing hell.

The Quantum rounds hit the hull, and exploded leaving gaping big craters. The fighter veered away.

Abe knew it would buy him a few precious minutes. He knelt back down in front of the torn power mounts and set back to work. His hands should have been shaking, but they were rock steady. He worked swiftly and efficiently in reconnecting the mounts so that the Jump Drive could operate. He felt sure of himself, of what he was doing.

Paul would have been a dead weight. And he was an unnecessary sacrifice. The replicants - the men and women inside - would need him. They didn't need a man like Abe to lead them. Not really. His days of warmongering were pretty much over. He could feel it. Now it was their turn to fight the Union. Their time for bloodshed. Whether they realised it or not. It would come.

He felt tired. Not of body or mind, or even of heart. But tired in the soul. Worn out. But he still had some fight in him, and as the enemy fighter appeared behind him, flanked on both sides by several other smaller fighters, he sprang up.

This time he didn't reach for the rifle.

He took a grenade, switched it from timed contactor to impact detonator. He waited for the other fighter to rise up behind the *Neberkenezer* then tossed the grenade at it. It drifted straight into the front window of the cockpit and exploded. The front of the fighter blew apart, broken. It spiralled.

Other fighters scrambled to avoid it. As it exploded fully it took two fighters with it.

Abe cackled at the destruction he had caused with a single grenade.

Just like old times, he thought.

* * *

"Hey! What was that?" Paul asked, peering past Stape to the front viewscreen.

"An explosion behind us. Maybe a couple. I don't know. It doesn't matter." Stape concentrated hard on every bit of debris coming their way.

Paul focused on the section of Drift ahead of them.

"I see space," he said.

That did catch Stape's attention, because he spared it a glance.

"Looks like it."

Paul looked up, and in almost a prayer he said "Come on Abe..."

* * *

Abe spotted the opening in the Drift nearing closer and closer.

Out of time.

Using both hands he pulled the two halves of the mounts together, squeezed them tight into each other. He opened the comm channel within his helmet.

"Court! Check the Drive!" he yelled.

"Nothing!" Court answered back.

"Fuck!" he shouted, turning back to the mounts in temper. "Why aren't you fucking working!?"

He pulled them apart again, ran a gloved finger over the end of one of the contacts. They were leaving the Drift now. Just getting through the last of it. He could see open space. He could almost taste it.

No time now. No fucking time.

"Work you cocksuckers," he spat, slamming them back together.

"Now?" he said into his helmet.

The *Neberkenezer* broke through the last of the Drift, and emerged into the deep blackness of space. If he could have breathed in the vacuum, Abe would have removed his helmet and filled his lungs with it.

Enemy fire struck the hull behind him, barely missing him. It just scratched the surface, but it was close. He shot a look behind to see three fighters closing in.

Shit, he thought.

And then something caught his eye. He glanced to the left. It was the Union battleship, a white colossus armed to the teeth bearing down on them.

In seconds it would be on top of them.

"We're good to go!" Court screamed down the other end.

There was no time to get back inside. No time for anything.

Well that's it, he thought.

"Hit it!" Abe yelled, standing up on the hull and spreading his arms wide apart.

Space beckoned. The light of every star shrank back and then expanded to infinity. Abe took one last deep breath, threw his head back. Closed his eyes. Smiled. Rode the wave as it took him.

The *Neberkenezer* made the Jump. Abe became one with the stars.

43.

It is getting lighter and lighter. He rises. The dark lifts him towards the light.

"Why leave me here?" she asks him. She reaches out to take his hand - his real one. This time he does not flinch away.

"You're staying with me?" she asks.

Abe smiles. Nods.

"I'll never leave you," he says.

He means it. More than he's ever meant anything.

"I love you Abe," she says.

He pulls her close to him, holds her, closes his eyes. "I love you too."

The dawn is coming. They turn to face it, together.

EPILOGUE

Extract from *A History Of The Terran Union, Volume XXII*
(Third Revised Edition)

"...although he was never seen or heard of again, the criminal known as *The Tattooed Man* had set the wheels in motion of something larger, a movement that would change the course of history. Twelve Terran months later, the self-styled *Full Metal Marquis* launched its first major offensive against a replicant production facility. In retrospect this first strike against the Union has been considered by many to be the start of the last great war of the Union, a conflict termed *The Marquis Wars*. Beginning in..."

END

AFTERWORD

I grew up on Sci-Fi. When I was a kid I'd wake every sunday morning to catch *Star Trek* re-runs on Channel 4. I loved the classic episodes. You know, the episodes like '*City At The Edge Of Tomorrow*' and '*Amok Time*' that everybody talks about. But I also liked the lesser, cheaper episodes from the show's third season.

'*All Our Yesterdays*' where Spock falls in love with Zarabeth. '*Return of the Archons*' where Kirk literally talks the ruling computer of the planet to death. '*The Savage Curtain*' where an alien life form calls forth figures from history to do battle. Kirk finds himself fighting alongside his hero Abraham Lincoln and Spock comes face to face with the saviour of his race, Surak.

All brilliant episodes, in my view. I watched *The Next Generation*, too, but it could never beat the fun and entertainment of *The Original Series* for me. There's something about that triangle of Kirk, Spock and Bones that just plain works. Emotion, Logic and Heroism.

After *Star Trek* I used to watch *Land Of The Giants*, which was great. And *Blake's 7*. For anyone who hasn't ever caught an episode of *Blake's 7*, it's required viewing. Sure, it's campy BBC Sci-Fi, but that's what's great about it.

If you like the old episodes of *Dr. Who* (I can't even watch the modern ones - shock! horror!) then I guarantee you will like *Blake's 7*. It follows an escaped prisoner, Blake, and the crew he puts together to stand against the evil Federation. It had a talking ship and everything. Watch it.

I didn't really get into *Star Wars* until the Special Editions. I was born in 1985, so I missed the original go-round of the series by about 10 years. The Special Editions were my education in the force, and over the summer of 1997 I went to the cinema to see all three. I loved them. When they released the VHS box set in gold and black for Christmas that year, you can probably guess what was on my list, right at the top.

I still have that box set. I don't even have a VHS player anymore. I just can't throw it away. Even now that I've got them on DVD and Blu-Ray, I can't part with those old tapes. I very nearly wore out The Empire Strikes Back I think, and it still remains as my favourite episode to this day.

After *Star Wars* I discovered *2001: A Space Odyssey* and even at the age of thirteen or fourteen my mind was just blown. I then went on to read all of the novels in the series by clarke, *2001, 2010, 2061* and *3001*. That then lead to me reading most of Clarke's stuff. *The Songs of Distant Earth, Childhood's End, The Fountains of Paradise, The Deep Range, The Ghost of the Grand Banks*, etc etc. I read anything by Clarke that I could get my greedy little mitts on. It's weird how things have a kind of domino effect.

I went from *Space Odysseys* to vast intergalactic empires in Isaac Asimov's *Foundation Series*. I also read most of his robot stuff. I learned that Asimov and Clarke were best of friends. I also learned that Clarke had been a friend of C.S. Lewis, whose *Chronicles of Narnia* I devoured as a kid. So I went and read his *Perelandra Trilogy* beginning with *Out Of The Silent Planet* (the same copy I have on my shelf today).

I read the Thrawn *Star Wars* books by Timothy Zahn, which led to me reading his *Conquerors* books. Then I read the *Star Wars* Jedi Apprentice books by Kevin J Anderson. Hmm. Good, but not great.

At some point I picked up *Star Trek: Ashes of Eden* by William Shatner and thought it was just brilliant (naive, I know). After reading several of the Shat's books I gave up on *Star Trek* in print. That is until years later when I stumbled across the *Star Trek: Crucible* series by David R. George. If you only ever read one *Star Trek* novel, just read the first *Crucible* novel. It spans literally all of *Star Trek*, and has a tragic love story to boot. What's great about it though, is that it works as an actual novel. If you did a find and replace on the names Kirk, Spock, Bones it wouldn't matter. It's a great book.

Now before I ramble on too much, I'll tell you where this is going.

My nan died in December 1999, and during that Christmas the BBC were showing a whole marathon of films. There was the original *Battlestar Galactica* movie, *The Final Countdown* with Kirk Douglas (a time travel escapade involving a modern aircraft carrier going back to the day of the Pearl Harbour attacks), and *Star Trek II: The Wrath Of Khan*. This wasn't the first time I'd seen *TWOK*, though.

When I was about 7, I had a black and white TV in my room. This was about

1992. It had four channels, and you had to turn a small red dial with a screwdriver to tune it in. One night my Dad shouted up the stairs for me to change the channel, a *Star Trek* film was on. I turned over, got into bed with the lights off and started watching. By the time the end credits were rolling, I was a wreck.

My brother died several years before, and I was just starting to understand it and make sense of it all. I'd been watching the re-runs of *Star Trek*, so I was more than familiar with Kirk and Spock. But seeing Kirk bid farewell to his friend like that... it opened something up inside of me that had never really healed back.

I know it sounds silly, but the film really has affected me in such a big way. I laid in bed that night, crying my eyes out. I felt real grief, and it was for my brother because I realised that I had witnessed the death of a brother on the screen. I was starting to understand how Kirk felt.

So those years later, following nan's death, I went through the same process. I was taping it onto VHS (remember when you could do that? Before tivo?) and I would end up watching that tape many, many times. *TWOK* helped me in not only understanding what had happened, but in moving on from it.

"He's not dead, so long as we remember him," Bones says in the film.

The film is famous for being the *Trek* film that really works. I mean REALLY works, on all levels. But to me there is a personal connection. It doesn't matter how many times I watch it, I truly feel the loss of Spock. The gravity of him passing on, and the void that is left without him there. As Spock says in *The Undiscovered Country*, "Nature abhors a vacuum." He's right. It really does. When people pass on you feel as though there is nothing in the world that will ever fill that hole. But eventually something moves in to claim the void. And somehow, over time, you are made whole again. Just one of nature's wonders, I guess.

I think I can honestly say that *Star Trek* has had the biggest impact on me, in terms of how I approach Sci-Fi. In *The Stars My Redemption*, I've drawn heavily on elements from many things. You could say that the technology present in the novel is more akin to what you'd find in *Star Wars*. That's true. I didn't want the reader to get bogged down in understanding how everything works. It just does, and that should be good enough. The story has a pulpy feel, and that too is intentional. I wanted it to be sharp and snappy, and writing it in the tradition of pulp (or my idea of it anyway) fit the bill perfectly.

The Stars My Redemption is the story of an amoral man - the most wanted man in the galaxy in fact - offered the chance at redemption. So there is gore, there is a lot of swearing. There's sex. But... there's a heart. And that heart, the emotions that I've tapped into in writing certain scenes of *The Stars My Redemption* all stem from that first experience watching *The Wrath of Khan*. It's how it connects to me.

I think that if it connects with me, and it brings a tear to my eye, then maybe it will bring a tear to yours.

And Abe?

When I thought about the character of Abe himself, I pictured a bald man with a white eye and a robotic arm that had seen more than his fair share of danger. I envisioned him covered in scars deep as tree bark and old tattoos from all four corners of the galaxy. A man who has literally been chewed to bits by the jaws of life. I thought that the uglier I made him outside, the more striking it would be to find that he still had a heart inside. As for his speech? He talks like some people I know or have come across. He's a common man, and I wanted him to have that common flavour when he spoke.

I hope that readers enjoy *The Stars My Redemption*, and that they want more. I can't say that there will be a sequel to the book. It's a stand-alone novel in many ways. But I've left myself plenty of room for another novel set in the same universe, so maybe readers will be seeing more. As for Abe, I can tell you that there will be individual short stories featuring him. I might even write a prequel. He has a lot of history, and there are many adventures that are yet to be revealed. How did he become the most wanted man in the galaxy? I think he did something very very bad, and I think I have an idea what that might have been.

But you'll have to wait to find out. My next novel is a thriller called *Adolf Hitler Must Die.* At the time of this writing I am halfway through it. I hope to publish it August 2012, all going well. I may even serialise it. But after that?

Maybe I'll look to the stars again. See what's going on.

Also by Tony Healey:

The Author Recommends:

SUPERBIA by Bernard Schaffer

NOBLE by David K. Hulegaard

WILD CHILDREN by Richard Roberts

STITCH by A. D. Bloom

DARKER BY DEGREE by Keri Knutson

PANDORA'S SUCCESSION by Russell Brooks

DISTANT MACHINES by Simon John Cox

GUARDING ANDREW GATES by Frank Zubek

Support Independent Publishing and leave a review for the books you enjoy!

www.fringescientist.com

www.tonyhealey.com

www.kindleallstars.com